Shifter

Wicked Woods #6

kailin gow

Shifter: Wicked Woods #6

Shifter
Published by Sparklesoup Inc.
Copyright © 2012 Kailin Gow

For information, please contact:

www.sparklesoup.com

DEDICATION

To my parents who were amazing enough to get a vacation property in a wooded mountain resort when I was a child where Wicked is based. Childhood memories and campfire tales are the stuff dreams are made of.

Prologue

Kevin had never thought he would be back at the werewolf king's mansion, not after all the games Josh had tried to play with him and Briony. Certainly not when he'd spent so much time stuck in Palisor. Yet here he was, not just in the Wickhams' house, but actually in Josh's office, his feet up on the antique desk while he read through another of the books Josh's sister Carol had brought out from Josh's hiding place.

Kevin brushed a strand of his long dark hair away from his face. There was no question about why Carol had done that, of course. Even now, sitting there in the large, old fashioned armchair that Josh used, Kevin could practically feel her eyes on him, mentally removing the plaid shirt and jeans he wore from the equation so that her imagination could focus on the muscles underneath.

He forced himself to concentrate on the book, because no matter how interested Carol was, he wasn't about to return that interest. Yes, she was beautiful, with an athletic body, deliciously perfect features, dark wavy hair, and probably the most direct gaze he'd ever seen in a girl, like a challenge every time she looked at someone. She was wearing a cut off t-shirt like the one she sported now, showing a lot of bare, toned stomach above the waistband of her jeans. She had heavy work boots on her feet that were like her, tough and practical. Aside from her trips to get more books, those didn't move. She was too busy standing there, just watching him.

Kevin didn't care. Briony was the one who mattered. Briony was the reason he was here, reading through Wickham family records dating back to the eighteenth century and beyond, to the time when they'd first arrived in Wicked. Which meant that even with Carol there, he could easily concentrate on the diary in front of him, looking for any mention of Palisor and its connection to the werewolves of Wicked.

Specifically, he found himself hoping that there would be something that would tell him why Josh was suddenly the only werewolf allowed into Palisor. With that information, maybe there would also be something that would tell him how to change that situation. If Briony was in Palisor, then he needed to be there too.

"You know," Carol said, "once Josh realizes how much power there is to be had in Palisor, he'll probably stay until he gets it."

She'd moved, seating herself on a big leather chair in the corner, her legs crossed delicately at the ankles. She looked almost sweet and demure like that, but neither word was one that really applied to a girl who would quite happily spend her day transforming into a wolf so that she could tear apart vampires. As for the way she generally reacted around Briony...

"You know that my brother's pretty relentless when it comes to getting what he wants, right?" she said.

Kevin looked over at her. "I guess that must run in the family."

Carol smiled. "Have I made a move on you since *she* left? No, because I know that you're so besotted with those pheromones she gives off that it won't make any difference yet."

"It isn't just pheromones, Carol," Kevin said, standing to put the book away. "I love her."

"I bet that's what Josh is saying too." Carol's smile turned a little more pointed. "What? It was pretty obvious when they left that he had a thing for her, and like I said, my big brother is pretty relentless when it comes to things he really wants."

Kevin snorted at that like he didn't think Josh had a chance, but the truth was that it wasn't easy to stay unruffled about that. Briony was off in another world with both the king of the werewolves and Kevin's vampire brother, Fallon. He was pretty sure that he was okay when it came to Fallon. Briony had made her choice when it came to them, and he didn't think that Fallon would stoop to manipulation or tricks to get her back.

Josh, though... Kevin had seen some of the manipulations he'd tried since Briony arrived in Wicked. What he would try on the other side of the gate was anyone's guess. The werewolf king wasn't evil, exactly, but he certainly had very few qualms when it came to getting what he wanted. So if he had his sights set on Briony, or even on Palisor... that was enough to make Kevin shudder.

Worse, the books he'd read so far weren't helping. "Carol," he asked, "do *you* know of any way I can get into Palisor? There has to be some way around this restriction of only one werewolf being allowed inside."

Carol shrugged. "Beats me. I never paid attention. There were always too many details."

"And you aren't just saying that to keep me here?" Kevin asked.

Carol shook her head, a flash of irritation flickering across her face. "I wouldn't do that to you. I know that if I did, I wouldn't have *any* chance. I just don't know. Josh is the one interested in family history, not me."

Great. Which meant that they were stuck with whatever was in the books, and whatever the other werewolves around Wicked knew. Which probably wasn't much, given how good Josh was at keeping secrets. Kevin bent his attention back to the books, hoping that even so, there would be something.

There was a knock at the door.

"Come in," Kevin said, and Carol stood up to let whoever it was in. Even though she was relentless when it came to pursuing him, even though she clearly didn't like

Briony and had nearly gotten them all killed on at least one occasion, she'd been the one who'd been prepared to help him with this.

The door opened to reveal the short, young looking figure of Briony's brother Jake. The young half breed vampire/werewolf would have looked out of breath, if vampires could look that way. He looked ruffled and edgy, moving about in place like he couldn't quite stand still. Obviously, whatever he'd come for had him agitated.

"What is it, Jake?" Kevin asked.

"It's Pietre," Jake said.

"Already?" Kevin guessed he should have expected it, now that Briony and Sophie, her aunt, were gone, but he hadn't thought it would be this soon. Pietre had only just escaped the battle that had left vampire leader Marcus dead and so many of his vampires destroyed, so Kevin had thought that they might have at least a little breathing space before he tried anything new in his efforts to control Wicked.

Jake nodded. "I just came from George's diner. Pietre's vampires are showing up in ones and twos through town, trying to scare people, but it looks like more of them are moving in fast. There's just you, me and the Preservation Society left to stop them."

Kevin understood. The Wicked Woods Preservation Society sounded like it ought to be concerned with stopping the demolition of historic buildings. Instead, it was as tough a collection of monster hunters as Kevin had heard about, but it was almost completely human. Against Pietre's vampires, that was a *big* disadvantage.

He thought for a moment or two and then stood up. "Josh left me in charge here, so it's time to be in charge. Carol?"

Carol looked up at him, not standing, but obviously paying attention. "What are you going to do, Kevin?"

"It's what *you're* going to do," Kevin said. "Go outside and find as many of the local wolves as you can. I want them ready to protect the town. My guess is that Pietre is trying for some kind of revenge on Wicked since he can't get what he wants. We aren't going to allow that."

"Are you sure about this?" Carol asked. "I mean, Josh would never have cared about just a bunch of *humans*."

"Well, I'm not Josh," Kevin shot back, "but I am in charge here."

Carol looked at him for a couple of seconds, and Kevin got the feeling that even that hadn't dented the way she felt. If anything, she looked like she wanted to rush over and kiss him right there and then.

"Yes," she said. "Yes, you are. I'll do that right away."

Jake went with her, leaving Kevin to clear away some of the mess of papers. After a few minutes, he went downstairs through the werewolves' ancient house, out onto the neatly maintained lawn. There had obviously been a lot of werewolves around, because something like a couple of dozen of them were standing on the lawn. Some, even most, were in human form, dressed in the kind of loose, tough clothing that was either easy to remove when they changed or which would stand up to the rigors of the transformation. A few were in their wolf forms, moving through the crowd with yips and barks.

All of them were watching him. All of them. A few of the younger women looked at him the way Carol had, while all the rest looked at him with something close to admiration. He knew that was because he was the strongest of them and their inner wolves respected that the way they would any other truly alpha male, but even so, it was disconcerting to have so many people looking to him for instructions. What would they see there? Would they see the dark haired, muscular guy a few inches taller than them, or would they just see their leader, and leave the real him out of it?

Was that what it was like for Josh when he was here? Standing there, knowing that whatever he said, the others would do it? No. Kevin shook his head. He wasn't the same as Josh. He would do *better* than Josh. He looked around, spreading his hands.

"Look, you all know me," he said. "You know who I am, and you know that Josh has left me in charge. Well, there's a problem in town. Vampires."

"Vampires." The word came as a collective murmur from the crowd. Werewolves hated vampires instinctively, but these ones had months of violence to draw on as well. Pietre and his vampires had tried their best to wipe them out.

"It's Pietre," Kevin said. "He and his vampires are in town, causing trouble. Now, I say he needs to be stopped."

A lot of the werewolves nodded.

"But I'm not going to make you do it," Kevin insisted. "I know how many of you have been hurt fighting the vampires. I know how many of us have lost family." He couldn't help looking over to Carol then. Her brother Brian and her twin brother Channing were both dead thanks to the vampires. "If anyone wants to stay here, they can."

"Why would we stay here?" one of the men at the front asked. "You're our leader. We go where you go."

"No, that isn't..." Seeing his expression, Kevin gave up. When it came to werewolves, there wasn't much point in trying to persuade them to make their own minds up about things. Instead, he pointed in the direction of Wicked. "Then let's go stop them!"

Around him, werewolves roared their support. A few of the transformed ones howled. And two dozen angry werewolves set off in the direction of Wicked, looking for a fight, simply because he'd told them to.

Chapter 1

Briony woke up slowly, staring at the ceiling above her as she did so. It was hard *not* to stare, because that ceiling was decorated with a mural of tall, elegant figures dancing and kissing, dressed in silken finery that covered the whole rainbow and celebrating in the middle of woodland. The fangs in their smiles made it clear what they were. Hugtandalfer, like her aunt, like her father. Like her.

Briony didn't want to sit up right then, because the bed she was in felt like lying on clouds. It was so soft and comfortable that Briony could barely bring herself to move enough to look around the room she was in, though that was just as opulent. The walls were stone, but that stone was a mixture of swirling varieties of marble, covered here and there with elaborate tapestries showing delicate rural scenes. The furniture in the room was ornate, carved with swirls, curves and spirals, then covered in gold leaf. There was enough room for plenty of it too, because the room was huge.

Briony got up then, and seeing a dress laid out at the base of the bed, put it on. It was a mostly cream dress with an intricately worked black and silver bodice and delicate silver stitching around the hem. She put it on, and it felt like it had been made for her. When she went over to a gilt framed mirror in one corner, the effect was spectacular. Although maybe that wasn't just the dress. Her hair shone like spun gold, falling loose almost to her waist. Her blue eyes shone back like sapphires and even her skin seemed to shine with them. Briony had known that she was good looking, but here, like this, she looked better than she ever had.

There was a set of double doors at one end of the room, opening out onto a balcony. Briony stepped out onto it, enjoying the feel of the sun on her skin, then looking down as she heard the roar of water beneath her. It took a moment to understand what she was seeing, because there were layers of what looked like mist between her and it, but then Briony saw it. A waterfall. Her balcony was directly above a waterfall that stood spectacularly high, water roaring over it, with the sunlight forming rainbows as it fell to whatever lay beneath.

Briony looked around more then, seeing smooth white stone standing above sheer white cliffs. A castle? While she'd been in castles before, they'd been nothing like this, and if she was in one, then that meant... she looked up to see the sky tinged as much with purple and gold as with blue. Palisor.

"So you're awake." Briony turned to see her great aunt staring at her. Not that Sophie looked much like a great aunt these days, since she'd come into her power as a hugtandalfer. She only appeared a year or two older than Briony now at most, with golden tanned skin and almost white blonde hair. She was wearing a dress like Briony's except that it was a deep emerald green. She was beautiful as she smiled.

"Palisor has sights that are like nowhere in the mortal world," Sophie said.

Briony nodded. "Nowhere I've seen, anyway. Where are we?"

"You don't remember? I guess you wouldn't. They call this the Cloud Palace. It was meant to be a retreat for royalty, built on the highest land in the kingdom. It's so high that even the clouds pass below."

Briony swallowed on hearing that. "Palisor again."

"You don't like it here, darling?" Sophie asked. It was strange sometimes, having her still say the kind of things a great aunt might say even when she looked more like an older sister.

"I was hoping..." Briony hesitated a little before actually saying it. "I like Palisor. It's beautiful, but part of me was hoping that I was still in Wicked with the Preservation Society. With Kevin. I was hoping that everything with Josh, and the betrothal and everything was just a bad dream."

Sophie put an arm around her shoulders. To Briony, it felt more comfortable, more like *home*, than anything had since she'd arrived back in the kingdom.

"I know," Sophie said. "If I'd known that the scepter and the people of Palisor could push you together with the werewolf king, I would have warned you, I swear."

Briony believed her, but it didn't do anything to change the situation they found themselves in. "Is Josh here too?"

The leader of the werewolves was older than her, college age, but everything a girl could have wanted in a man. He was handsome, charming, with preppy good looks and the charisma to persuade people to do what he wanted. He clearly cared about both his siblings and his people, and he was ruthless enough to stand up to a dangerous world. He would have made a good king, even a good husband. Just not for her. Never for her. Briony simply didn't love him.

"You have a choice, darling," Sophie assured her. "They can't make you marry Josh. You might be the heir to the kingdom, but you could still walk away. You could still reject it, and Josh with it. Or Vigor, if he wants you to push a blood claim to the throne."

Vigor was kind of like Briony's step-brother, taken in by the king as a suitable candidate for the throne. His only disadvantage was that he didn't have any real royal blood, or the connection to the scepter at the heart of Palisor's power that came with it. He was handsome and strong, in a blunt, no nonsense way.

Briony smiled. "I thought he was more interested in you."

Sophie returned her look. "I think maybe he is, but for the throne of Palisor? To help the kingdom, as he sees it? He'll want you. And then there's Fallon, of course."

"Fallon's here," Briony said brightly. "At least I have that."

Fallon. She loved him. She had been torn between Kevin and his vampire brother Fallon for so long. She loved both of them, and at one point, she thought she may have loved Fallon as much as Kevin. There was no doubt she cared for him, though. Enough to come here looking for a way to help him. Her mind raced, thinking about the possibilities.

"Sophie, I told Fallon we'd find a cure for him…a way to turn him back into human. There are stories… I heard something from Marcus' vampires about how when the scepter is found and placed back into the hands of the rightful heir in Palisor, the prophecy can be fulfilled. Marcus' brother said that was the reason why vampires try to cross into Palisor in the first place; to find their vampire paradise, to get their dreams fulfilled… to become human again."

"I hope so," Sophie said.

"Me too." Fallon was at the door. He looked beautiful, slender, golden haired and perfect as he stood there. He was still wearing modern clothes, dark jeans and

Kailin Gow

a hooded top, and those made him look out of place against the old fashioned splendor of the palace.

"I'll leave you alone with Briony to figure it out," Sophie said, stepping past the young vampire with a smile. Briony suspected that Sophie would have liked Briony to choose Fallon, if it was up to her. When had Wicked's most dangerous vampire hunter gotten to like him enough for that?

Fallon didn't wait, hurrying over and taking Briony into his arms. He kissed her, his tongue entwining with hers in a kiss so searing, she couldn't help kissing him back for a second or two before she pulled back.

"Briony," Fallon said, breathlessly, moving his lips down to her neck and her shoulders. His gaze drifted over to the bed. "Finally, I get a chance to be alone with you."

Briony shook her head gently. "No. We can't."

"You don't want to?" He nibbled at her ears, causing her to arched her back closer to his chest, while his hands pulled her closer. He turned her around until his lips captured hers and they continued kissing more passionately as Fallon led her gently to the foot of her bed.

"I want to *help* you," Briony said. "I want... I have the scepter now. I want to help you, and I can actually do some good here in Palisor."

"Haven't you done enough for everyone else?" Fallon said. "I know you're thinking about this crazy plan of Josh's just because it would be what's best for the kingdom, but what about what's best for *you*?" He searched her face earnestly. "What do *you* want?"

How had he managed to turn it around to that? Briony wasn't sure. She wasn't even sure that she had an answer. "I can't help myself. The people here see me as the blood heir. Even the scepter reacts like I am."

"And what does that mean?" Fallon asked.

Briony tried to look like she'd made her mind up. "I have to fulfill this prophecy. I have to find out what I'm meant to do with the scepter. There has to be more to it than just having it, or so many people wouldn't have died over it. My father…"

She tried not to think about finding King Waltham after Marcus' vampires had attacked to try to take the scepter.

"I know," Fallon said. He looked thoughtful for a second or two. "I've been trying to find out more about the scepter, trying to help, but… well, I'm a vampire among the fanged elves. I get the feeling that it's hard enough for most of them not to try killing me."

"I'm just glad you're here," Briony said. She kissed him, gently, even though she knew she probably shouldn't, as confused as she was, with loving both him and his brother Kevin.

"At least I'm in the same world as you this time." Unlike Kevin, Briony couldn't help thinking with a tiny stab of something close to pain. Fallon kept going. "I don't care who they think you should marry. I don't care about anything. I love you, and I'm going to do everything I can to be with you."

"Everything?" Josh asked from the doorway.

Briony was starting to wish that the doors were locked, but that was one of the things about being a ruler in a castle like this. Privacy was something that happened to other people. She tried to compose her features as she looked at Josh, trying to keep her expression polite and composed even though the king of the werewolves had more or less set her up when they'd come here. He'd known that only one werewolf would be allowed into Palisor, but he'd also guessed that it would put him in a good position to become her consort and gain power there.

The trouble was, it was difficult to stay angry looking at Josh. He was a very handsome man with short brown hair and well defined, athletic features. He had the body to go with it, not as heavily built as some of his brothers, maybe, but still strong and good looking. He'd found a light colored tunic and hose to wear that came close to matching Briony's dress. She found herself wondering if that was deliberate.

"What are you doing here, Josh?"

Josh laughed. "A deal is a deal, Briony. You've fulfilled yours. But I've yet to fulfill mine. I thought I should."

Briony tried not to look surprised at that. Of course Josh would keep his word. That was the thing about him. He could manipulate people one moment and be a perfectly nice guy the next. He wasn't evil like Pietre, he just liked to make sure things turned out his way. He had also been a good ally to her and the Preservation Society against the vampires who terrified the Wicked Woods.

"What do you mean by keeping your word?" Briony asked, wanting to check anyway.

Josh nodded as if he'd been expecting her to say that. "I'm going to help you find the power in Palisor to get rid of both the vampires here and those back in Wicked, of course. Together we're going to make sure that your people don't have to worry about vampires like Marcus again, while mine will be safe from Pietre. We're going to do it, Briony. Together."

Chapter 2

Kevin ran with the rest of the werewolves following him, eating up the ground in his wolf form, the distance disappearing in easy strides. Beside him, Carol's dark furred wolf form kept pace with him, while on the other side the smaller form of Jake bounced along, keeping up despite the difference in their sizes. The rest of the werewolves from Wicked's pack followed behind him, and that was a strange kind of feeling, but a powerful one. All those wolves were following *him*, ready to fight just because he'd ordered it, looking to him for orders.

They came to the edge of the trees near the town, transforming back into human form and adjusting clothes rumpled or torn by the change. Carol reached over, starting to straighten out Kevin's shirt, and Kevin pulled back, even though he could see the hurt look that he got from her.

He had other things to concentrate on right then though as they made their way to the diner, walking down Wicked's quiet streets. Things like the danger to all the people he'd come to know at George's diner. They were good people there, all members of the Preservation Society, all trying their best to make sure that the town stayed safe from threats like Pietre and other human-hating vampires.

The diner came into sight. It had an old fashioned look to it, like someone might be able to walk in from nineteen fifty and feel right at home, with a big sign out front saying *George's*, the big windows showing an interior with booths and tables spread out in front of the counter, and the pictures on the walls that Kevin couldn't see at this distance but he knew mostly showed moments from George, the owner's life. Though not from his life as a vampire after he'd been turned by Pietre.

The hardest part about being at the diner was the people who weren't there. People, he admitted to missing. Briony should have been there, waiting on tables and smiling at customers as they tipped her. Her great aunt should have been there too. Despite himself, Kevin liked Mrs. Edge a lot now that she'd gone from hunting both vampires and werewolves to focusing on the fight against the vampires. Even as an old woman, she'd been able to fight better than almost anyone thanks to her hugtandalfer heritage. Now that she had transformed, it would have been useful to have her around for the fight to come. Her and Briony, two of the best vampire slayers in Wicked.

But they weren't here, which meant that it was up to him and the other werewolves to defend the diner against Pietre's vampires. Kevin's eyes narrowed slightly as he thought of that. Pietre had attacked them so many times, in so many different ways. He was going to make the vampire pay for his constant harassment of the town. He and the other werewolves got closer to the diner, spreading out in a rough line to defend it.

"I can smell vampires," Carol said beside him. There was anger there that didn't quite disguise the trace of fear in her scent. Kevin knew she wouldn't be scared of the fight itself, but she'd been captured and tortured by the vampires once. That kind of thing left a mark.

"It's going to be fine, Carol."

"I don't need a pep talk," she snapped back. That was her. She'd always rather be angry than scared.

"Do you think the diner's defenses are working?" Jake asked.

Kevin thought. They'd had holy water sprinklers and more there before, for the last attack. Would those be ready again?

"We can't take the chance," he said. "Just remember to keep out of the way of any holy water that does come your way, Jake."

"I'll be fine," the boy promised. "What I want to know is where Pietre's vampires are. I can smell them, but they aren't here."

Kevin nodded. Here on the street, he could smell them too. Yet the only vampire he saw in the next few seconds was George, the diner's grey haired, fifty something owner, who stepped out onto the street with a questioning look. He was a well-built man who had spent some time in the military, and still had that sense of crisp neatness about him, even wearing casual slacks, a shirt with its sleeves rolled up and a cook's apron over the top.

"What's going on here, Kevin?" he asked. "You aren't all here for lunch, I guess?"

"We heard that Pietre was causing trouble in town," Kevin said. "We heard he was heading here. Wait, why don't you know that?"

There was something wrong there. Something very wrong. That's when the first howl of pain went up from the end of their defensive line. Another quickly followed.

"Someone stabbed Chris," Carol said, looking down the line. "Where are they coming from?"

Kevin didn't know. He looked around, trying to figure it out. "Everybody watch your backs. No, better than that, every second person turn around. I don't want anyone sneaking up on us."

"This close to the diner?" one of the werewolves asked.

"Just do it," Kevin ordered. There wasn't enough time to stand there and debate it. Not with his werewolves getting hurt. Three of those who had come were on the ground. He didn't know how badly injured they were. But how could vampires get close to them without being seen…

Kevin found himself remembering Pietre's trick of appearing and disappearing, wrapping the shadows around himself so it seemed like he was invisible. Could he have somehow taught that trick to other vampires? *Would* he have, since it was something they could just as easily use against him? There was only one way to find out.

Kevin looked down the line, checking the end of it where the three werewolves had been hurt. There was a wall casting a long shadow there. Kevin walked towards it, trying to look like he was just checking on the injured wolves, but actually straining his senses.

That was why, when a vampire appeared in the shadow of the diner halfway there, he was ready. He caught the arm holding the knife that swung towards him, breaking it effortlessly and catching the silver blade as it dropped. He stabbed the vampire once, then again, striking the heart. He had a brief instant to look at the vampire, which seemed to be no more than a high school kid in a t-shirt and cut of jeans, before it died and blue fire leapt up to consume it.

That wasn't the only thing that leapt up. Vampires appeared from the shadows, charging forward at the wolves. One leapt at Jake, and the smaller wolf dealt with it easily, but when a second tried to join in, Kevin jumped forward to intercept it. Her. It was a girl maybe Briony's age, with cheerleader good looks and blonde hair tied back in pigtails like she was deliberately trying to be cute. Maybe that was what made Kevin pause just long enough for fangs to sink into his neck.

With a roar of pain, he shoved the vampire back. He leapt forward, transforming into a wolf mid leap and tearing at the vampire. He managed to get a grip on her neck, snapping it easily, then letting go as her body started to burn to ash. He looked around for the next vampire. There were plenty to choose from, though his werewolves seemed to be handling them. Kevin threw himself at another of the previously invisible attackers.

Again, he quickly slipped in, got a grip on the vampire's neck and ended it. It was easy. Almost *too* easy. Kevin pulled back from the fight, changing back into human form and trying to think. Vampire after vampire was falling to his werewolves, but there was still no sign of Pietre. He looked around at the vampires still fighting, too, and he could see just how young they had to be. Newly made, and mostly, it seemed, from high school age kids. In fact, he thought he recognized one or two. Hadn't they been in his classes when he was a substitute there?

That was almost enough for him to tell his wolves to leave them, but he knew he couldn't. They were vampires, eager to feed on humans. They had to be stopped. More came towards them, openly this time, heading down the street. Again, they seemed to be no more than kids.

Jake was there beside him. "They're newly turned," he said. "My vampire side can sense that. They can't be more than a few hours old, if that."

"Pietre must have turned them, one after another," Kevin guessed. "That's just... sick, doing that to kids."

Jake nodded. He'd know better than anyone. At only fourteen, Pietre had turned him. "I guess it explains why he'd teach them how to disappear," he said. "He can't think that they'd survive a fight with us, and even if they do, then they still won't be powerful enough to be a problem for him."

"So why send them against us?" Carol asked, changing back into human form and finishing off a dark haired girl who was writhing in pain on the ground.

"As a distraction," Kevin guessed. "He's obviously sent the first batches of new vampires to keep us busy."

"While he does what?" Carol insisted.

One possibility came to Kevin. "He lost a lot of vampires in Marcus' scheme. The ones who weren't trapped in Palisor were mostly killed in the battles after that. What if he's trying to build up his followers again, and using the school to do it? He's sent these ones this way, then maybe he and his remaining vampires are at the school, making more like them?"

"But that's..." It seemed even Carol didn't have the words for it. Maybe she was just thinking about how easily it could have happened to her if she hadn't been a werewolf. "We have to stop them."

Kevin nodded. He pointed to four of the werewolves still there. "You four, stay here and protect the diner. The vampires that come this way shouldn't be strong, but they might come out of the shadows, so stay alert. Try to help the three who are wounded too. The rest of you, come with me."

"Where are we going?" one of the remaining werewolves asked.

"We need to get over to the high school," Kevin said. "Now hurry, but stay in human form. We've probably shocked enough people for one day."

"I doubt they're that shocked anymore," Carol pointed out. "After all the fights there have been around Wicked between us and the vampires, I'd be surprised if even stupid humans could keep pretending we don't exist."

"Carol…"

"What?" she demanded. "I didn't say I wouldn't *help* them, did I? If you want me at the high school, or anywhere else, that's where I'll go."

Kevin shook his head. "It shouldn't be just because I want you to do it, Carol."

Carol shrugged. "Do you really have time for a debate? I thought we were in a hurry."

They were, so Kevin started to run. The rest of the werewolves ran with him, heading for the school. He just hoped that they wouldn't be too late. Except of course, for so many of the students Pietre had transformed, they already were.

Chapter 3

Running over, Kevin was briefly concerned that they might not be able to get into the school easily; that the high school's security would see him with what appeared to be a gang of rough looking, disheveled individuals and refuse to let them inside, even if he was a former teacher there. He'd thought that it might have caused problems, having to knock them out to get in.

Yet one look at the school told him that they had much bigger things to worry about. The large, slightly dated buildings of Wicked's high school were quiet in a way that full school buildings never truly were. Ordinarily, there would have been at least a few kids out in between classes, or running because they were late, or just hanging out in one of the large open spaces nearby. Now though, there was nothing. Even the small security hut on the gate was quiet, though Kevin quickly scented the reason for that. When he looked inside, there was a middle aged man in a security uniform, dead and bloodless. Kevin motioned the wolves with him past the gate.

That was when a second security guard leapt out from the shadows beside the gate, throwing himself at Kevin. Kevin didn't even hesitate. He grabbed the man, who in life had been bulky and muscular but who was too young in vampire terms to be truly strong, and slammed him back against the security hut. Kevin hit him once, twice, and then grabbed him, stepping behind the man to pin his arms.

"Where are they?" he demanded.

The guard opened his mouth wide, showing fangs as he tried to turn his head to bite Kevin. Carol stepped forward and broke his neck, then shoved a piece of wood that looked like a chair leg from one of the chairs in the guard hut into him. The vampire guard died without a sound.

"What did you do that for?" Kevin demanded.

"He was going to bite you," Carol shot back. "Besides, you know he wouldn't have said anything useful.

You probably know as much about where they'll be as he did."

Annoyingly, Carol was probably right. There were only so many places that the vampires could use if they wanted to keep a large number of students in one spot. Of those, some offered the vampires better opportunities to control the students than others.

"The gym," Kevin declared. "They'll be in the gym."

"There," Carol said, reaching up to put a hand on his shoulder. "You see, I was right."

"Just... don't kill anyone else without my say so," Kevin ordered.

Carol looked away. "Yes, my king."

"I'm not anyone's king," Kevin said.

Carol shrugged. "Maybe you should be."

Kevin ignored that, leading the way to the school's gym, he crept forward quietly, signaling to the other werewolves to keep low. Most of them did that by transforming, padding along silently behind him. They couldn't afford to alert the vampires to their presence. Not that Kevin believed the vampires would be able to stop them, but if they were in the school, then there was too much of a chance that they would have kids nearby, and Kevin knew Pietre wouldn't hesitate to hurt any hostages he had if he saw the werewolves coming.

So they moved as quietly as they could around the side of the school gym, working their way to the entrance. There was a figure there, standing out in the open. Carol started forward, but Kevin put a hand on her shoulder.

"What?" she asked.

"The guard on the gate wasn't in plain view like that." He stopped, sniffing the air and then shifting shape as easily as breathing. In his wolf form, the colors of the world faded to black and white, but his other senses were so much sharper. He shifted back, looking over to Jake. "Do you sense him?"

"The other one?" Jake asked. He nodded.

"Take him when I take the obvious one then," Kevin said. He changed again, creeping forward until he was in striking range of the young man, the vampire, on the door. His muscles bunched and he leapt.

One on one, werewolves were stronger than vampires. The problem was always finding a way to actually kill them. Tearing them apart completely might work, but generally it was a question of attacking the neck and hoping for the best. The trouble was that most vampires who saw the attack coming protected their throats instinctively. In this case though, Kevin didn't have to worry about that. He hit the vampire in front of him perfectly, his jaws closing on its throat, killing it in silence.

A second figure appeared, a girl who opened her mouth as if to scream a warning to the vampires inside. She didn't get the chance. Jake hit her from the side, his smaller but still powerful jaws clamping down to end her existence.

Kevin shifted back and opened the door to the gym just a crack. What he saw inside made his stomach knot in anger.

There were kids in the bleachers. Dozens of them, maybe more. Several classes' worth at least. They huddled together in quiet groups, whispering to one another, or praying, or just looking terrified as they had to watch what was going on down on the basketball court. There were vampires there. Old vampires. They stood around in a half circle on the three point line, and there were students on the floor beside them. One was bent over a girl who looked to be around Briony's age, his fangs sunk deep into her throat. Another, a female vampire, had her wrist out over the mouth of a boy who didn't seem any older than Jake, blood dripping from it as she forced him to drink in turn.

Pietre stood at the heart of it all, looking so ordinary. So utterly banal. The master vampire appeared to be in his early forties, and he wasn't handsome. He wasn't stunning. His hair was short and neatly cut, and he wore a suit that had probably cost a small fortune, but the overall effect was of the manager of some small business, not of one of the most powerful creatures of evil in the area.

In this case, he was a manager overseeing a kind of horrific production line. One by one, the vampires there drained their victims, giving them back blood, only to move onto another student plucked from the bleachers, and another. Kevin heard a low growl beside him, looking down to see Jake there, peering under his arm at the scene.

"We have to stop them," Jake whispered, and for a moment Kevin could hear the pain there. The pain that came from having been changed into a monster at such a young age, and knowing that he would never, ever, be any older than he was now.

"We will," Kevin promised. He slipped back outside to the other werewolves. "Jake and I are going inside," he said. "When it starts, you all have just one job, and that is to get the kids out of there."

"Our job is to keep you alive," Carol countered, "not to protect a bunch of humans."

Kevin looked at her until she flinched. "A minute ago, you were calling me your king. I'm not that, but I *am* in charge here. Which means you'll get those kids out. Or do you *want* Pietre to populate Wicked with an army of transformed school kid vampires?"

He put that in so it wouldn't just be about giving her an order, but he could see that he didn't need to. From the moment he gave her a command, Carol was nodding, and so were the other werewolves. Again, it seemed to be enough for them that he was an alpha wolf, although maybe it was more than that with Carol. Maybe he should be careful when it came to that.

There wasn't the time to think about that then though. They had to act before Pietre could condemn more kids to an un-life of eternal darkness. Taking a deep breath, Kevin threw himself through the door to the gym, running forward at Pietre and the vampires with him, transforming as he ran.

He hit the first of them, the woman, as she was straightening up from feeding blood to the boy. His paws struck her in the chest, knocking her sprawling. With so many vampires though, Kevin couldn't follow that attack up, so he spun, ripping at the next of the vampires. Jake shot past him to attack another of them.

Kevin shifted, turning to land a kick on the knee of a vampire approaching him, followed by a punch to the jaw that had the creature briefly reeling. He saw Jake's teeth clamp down on the throat of one of the newly risen vampires, killing it before it could even join the fight.

There were more dangerous things to worry about than new vampires though. Pietre swept forward, his nails lengthening to their familiar, knife-like length. He swiped at Kevin, and Kevin reacted by shifting forms to throw his weight against Pietre's legs. The master vampire fell, but one of his fellow vampires was there, swinging a foot at Kevin's side so fast that he barely got out of the way. He spun, then changed direction to attack a third vampire who was trying to break free of the brawl to stop the young people who were starting to stream from the hall. Kevin caught his throat in his jaws, crushing it.

He changed back as Pietre attacked with strike after strike, but Kevin managed to get out of the way. Finally though, he pulled back.

"If I wanted to," he said, "I could have my vampires tear you apart."

"I doubt it," Kevin replied. "You lost too many vampires in the battle by the gate. You don't want to lose more, and I have my wolves."

He didn't have to gesture. The other werewolves were just there, beside him.

"Then we will have to make it another time," Pietre said. "I can't waste time here." He looked around at the vampires with him. "We're leaving," he continued. "Go into the town. Take any humans you can. The end is coming, and we need as many vampires as we can to fight them."

"Who?" Kevin asked. "The hugtandalfer?"

Pietre snorted. "You really are a fool, wolf. I'm not worried about them. I'm worried about what they control. What will be unleashed if they come here. When Palisor has an heir, the scepter, and a powerful consort for the heir, creatures will come that will make mere fanged elves look like nothing. I will not let my children be destroyed."

Kevin smiled. "I don't think you get a choice about that."

"Oh, I do," Pietre promised. "With enough vampires… but why am I wasting time talking to you? It's time to do what I should have done decades ago. By this time a day or two from now, every human in Wicked will be one of my kind. Then what will you do, wolf?"

Kevin started to lunge forward at Pietre, but he was too slow. The master vampire leapt back, wrapping the shadows around him. One by one, his vampire followers did the same. Soon, they had vanished completely, leaving Kevin and the rest of his werewolves alone in a gym full of frightened students.

"Do you think it's true?" Carol asked him. "Do you think something big is happening?"

Kevin shrugged. "Even if it isn't, you heard Pietre. Unless we stop him, we'll have a whole town full of vampires to deal with."

Chapter 4

Briony looked from Fallon over to Josh, trying to judge the werewolf king's expression. Josh was impossible to read right then though.

"When you say 'deal with the vampires'…" Briony said.

"I mean that we can destroy them," Josh replied, apparently unconcerned that Fallon was right there. "There is the power in Palisor to destroy all of them, if only we have the courage to unleash it. If only we have the strength to do what we need to do for both our worlds."

"*All* the vampires?" Briony asked.

Josh nodded. "All of them, all at once. Imagine it, Briony."

Oh, she was imagining it, all right, and with some vampires, the thought of them being gone just like that was an appealing one. If they had a way to stop Pietre, for example… Yet the way Josh put it, it sounded like they wouldn't be able to choose which vampires were killed. Which meant that Fallon would be every bit as vulnerable. And what about George, down at the diner? What about *Jake*? Her brother might be half werewolf, but he still had plenty of vampire blood in him. Could Josh really be suggesting something that might kill Jake?

Briony stared at him, trying to understand how he could say it. Trying to work out what he had planned. Josh just stood there, looking like he was enjoying her gaze on him, and seeming as comfortable in the opulence of the palace as if he'd been born to it.

"This is why you talked me into bringing you over into Palisor, isn't it? You've known about this all along?"

Josh nodded. "I've known what the prophecy says, and I've known what we need to do to bring about the end of the vampires. I've known what we need to do ever since I first found out what you were."

"And what's that, Josh?" Briony demanded. "What do you think we need to do? What have you been planning all this time? Why did you really come to Palisor?"

Josh smiled then, and it seemed such a simple, straightforward smile. Yet Briony knew there was nothing either simple or straightforward about the werewolf king.

"Isn't it obvious, Briony?" he asked. "I came here to marry you."

"What?" Briony said in simple shock. "No! No way! I mean… you can't actually *mean* that, Josh. Why would you possibly think that I'd marry you?"

That made a spark of annoyance flicker across Josh's features.

"And why would you want to marry me?" Briony added. "I thought you were the one guy around me who genuinely wasn't interested in me that way."

Josh laughed then. "Oh, I wouldn't go that far, Briony. Those pheromones you put out are pretty appealing, especially to an alpha male drawn to a mate, and you're a beautiful girl. I'm not blind."

"Yet," Fallon said softly from Briony's side. He clearly didn't like the way the conversation was going.

Josh took a step forward. "Don't threaten me, vampire. Not here. I'm a werewolf in Palisor. You know what that means? One bite. One tiny bite, and it's over.

And even if that didn't do it, who do you think the hugtandalfer would side with? Me or you?"

"I think they'd side with their queen, Josh," Briony said, pushing him back with one hand. "So you need to stop trying to pick fights with people I care about. You haven't even answered my question yet. Why would you think we're going to get married?"

"Because you want the vampires stopped as much as I do," Josh said. He caught Briony's pushing hand and held it, turning it over to lower his lips to the palm. The movement was soft and unexpectedly sensual, causing Briony to gasp in surprise. "Because it will give power back to the hugtandalfer in Palisor, save the people of Wicked from the creatures that have been terrorizing them for centuries, and finally fulfill the prophecy."

Briony tried to force herself to think. "You mentioned this 'prophecy' before. Tell me about it. Stop playing games and just tell me what it says."

Josh shrugged. "Who's playing games?"

"Josh."

Josh half closed his eyes as though reciting from memory. "When the rightful heir to Palisor marries her powerful consort and the scepter is in her hand, then a great power will be unleashed to wipe the vampires from the land." He opened his eyes again. "I guess rhyming was compulsory in prophecies in those days, but this is our chance, Briony."

"So you want me to marry you because of one piece of bad poetry?" Briony demanded.

Josh put his hands on her shoulders, turning her away from Fallon, forcing her to focus on him. "I want you to marry me because the prophecy is true. I'm sure of it. I can feel it."

"You can *feel* it?" Fallon asked from the side.

Josh appeared to ignore him, focusing on Briony instead. "Is it so hard to believe that it might be true, Briony? They prophesized that you'd find the scepter, didn't they? They said that the rightful heir to Palisor would find it, and you did."

"I found it because it called out to me," Briony countered. "Not because of some prophecy."

Josh shook his head. "And why do you think it called out to *you* rather than someone else? Because you were meant to have it. Because you were meant to have the power that goes with it. The power to reshape Palisor and rid it of the vampires, if you can only unlock it. You know that power is there. You know that you have a connection to that power. Why is it so hard to believe that the rest of it might be true as well?"

That was the problem. When Josh explained it like that, so carefully, so reasonably, it was easy to see how it might be true. After all, she'd only gone looking for the scepter because she'd thought it might have the power to help Fallon. So why couldn't it also have the power to destroy vampires?

"If what you're saying is true," Briony asked, "then why didn't the kings and queens before me destroy the vampires? Are you telling me that none of them had powerful consorts and the scepter?"

Josh shrugged. "Maybe they did and maybe they didn't. Maybe they figured that it was enough to just drive back the vampires, or maybe they weren't prepared to do what they had to do to make both of the worlds safe. It doesn't *matter*, Briony."

Briony smiled. "But you know what does matter, right?"

"What matters is that we can make our worlds better, and do it so easily," Josh insisted. "We need to get married, Briony. We *have* to get married."

Briony shook her head. "No, we don't, Josh. Did you really think it would work like that? That you'd trick me by keeping this kind of news from me, demand that we get married, and then we'd both live happily ever after? I thought you were cleverer than that. You have to know that I can't do this."

"Why not?" Josh demanded. "I thought you'd want this as much as I do. Oh, I know you aren't in love with me, but what does that have to do with anything? True rulers have to put their feelings aside when it comes to the good of their kingdoms. I thought you knew that. Or are you still some silly little girl hoping that everything will be fine rather than working to make it happen?"

Briony stepped back from him. "You aren't making any friends here, Josh."

Josh seemed to struggle with himself for a moment, but then stopped. "Maybe you're right. Maybe I could have handled this better. But can't you see how important it is,

Briony? Can't you see how much good it would do to marry me?"

The hard part was that she *could* see it. She could see just how much getting rid of the vampires would change things, both for Palisor and in Wicked. People could live normal lives again, without the constant fear of being dragged into the darkness and fed upon. The Preservation Society wouldn't face a constant war against creatures too fast and strong to stop. Everyone could go back to normal. *Almost* everyone.

"If we did this, what would happen to Fallon? To Jake? All the vampires who have worked so hard not to feed on people?"

Josh shook his head. "You know what would happen, Briony."

"And you're okay with that?" Briony demanded.

"The vampires have taken everything from me," Josh snapped back. "*Everything.* I've lost my parents, my brothers. I've lost the life I had planned out for myself because I had to come back to Wicked to fight them. I've been forced into battles and I've had to send my people to their deaths against them. All that, because vampires were out there. I thought you'd feel the same way."

"Why?" Briony asked. "Because I lost my parents? Pietre made them vampires, Josh. If he hadn't staked them afterwards, this would have killed them too. It *will* kill my brother. So how can I feel the same way?"

Josh looked her in the eye. "Aren't you sick of the constant fighting? Aren't you sick of never having the life you wanted? You didn't sign up for any of this, Briony, and neither did I. This could end it."

"It could kill some good people," Briony shot back.

Josh raised his voice for the first time. "You didn't seem to care about that when you were sending my wolves to die battling the vampires! Your precious town needed protecting and you came to me with your aunt without a second thought. You spent the lives of my people like they didn't matter, but now it might be someone close to *you,* you aren't prepared to go through with it."

Briony reached out to put a hand on his shoulder. She could feel Josh actually tremble with his anger. Or maybe not just with anger. "I'm sorry, Josh. I know what you're saying, but I just can't do it. I *won't* do it."

Josh shrugged. "I don't think you're going to get a choice."

Briony shook her head, holding out an arm to stop Fallon as the vampire started forward. "You can't force me to marry you."

"I can't, but your people might. The scepter has already chosen me as your consort. And then there's the question of the gates. Can you control them yet, Briony? Fully control them?"

"I opened and closed the gates to bring us here," Briony pointed out.

"And then you couldn't open it again. You still don't have full control over the kingdom. You need to unlock the power of the scepter for that."

"So you've backed me into a corner," Briony said.

Josh nodded. "That's what politics is. Being pushed and pulled in directions you don't want, trying to make the best of it. *I* know. I know that better than anyone. Do you think I wanted to be a king?"

"So you're going to make Briony suffer because your life didn't turn out the way you wanted?" Fallon demanded.

"I'm not going to do anything now," Josh said. "Because when we're married, I want us to be happy. I'm not going to force Briony into this. But Briony, you need to start thinking. Without the power of the scepter... well, how are you ever going to get home to see all those people you care about so much? If you ever want to see them again, you'll marry me."

Chapter 5

Kevin rushed with Jake back towards George's Diner, leaving Carol behind with the other werewolves at the school to deal with everything that had happened there. It wasn't ideal, but maybe having to help out a bunch of frightened kids would at least remind Carol that people who weren't werewolves still mattered. Maybe. After that, Kevin had left her with instructions to head back to the mansion and wait for him. With this new threat from Pietre, they couldn't take the risk of straying away from home.

It seemed, when they got to the diner, that George had taken the same attitude. Outside, the holy water sprinklers were running, sending up sprays of water that Jake had to dart between. Inside, there were dozens of people, far more than would normally have been there in the middle of the day. Kevin recognized a lot of them as members of the Preservation Society, their vampire killing weapons carried openly now, but there were other people there too. Ordinary people, probably, who had just found out how dangerous their town really was.

Maisy and Steve were there too. Briony's two geek friends were sitting at one of the diner's tables with a small pile of weaponry between them, apparently arguing good naturedly over which of them was better with them.

"How can you be better than me with a crossbow when you're wearing glasses?" Steve pointed out. He'd cut his dark hair shorter recently, and seemed to have lost some of the slender softness that he'd had when Kevin first met him. Apparently, the fight against the vampires had been good for him. Or maybe it was just that he wanted to look good for Maisy.

"I think it must just be that I have better hand eye coordination than you do," Maisy countered. She kept her dark hair tied back in pigtails, her round glasses doing a lot to mask actually quite pretty features. Like Steve, she seemed a little fitter, a little harder, than she had when Kevin had first met her. All the fighting with vampires and running around in the woods have strengthened them in more ways than physically.

"What are you two doing here?" Kevin asked.

Maisy answered. "We were heading over to school after a study break when we saw the vampires. There were too many to fight, and this seemed like the best place to defend."

"When in doubt, run away," Steve added. It probably wasn't just a personal motto. The Preservation Society had survived as long as it had mostly by knowing that in a fair fight, there was no chance of its members winning against vampires. That was why they didn't fight fair.

Actually, Steve and Maisy had helped to change that a little. Neither one was much in a fight, but they were both clever, they'd both watched far too many sci-fi series, and Steve in particular liked to tinker with things. The result was that the Preservation Society now had more than a few inventive toys that might just allow its members to fight vampires more smartly. Like the sprinklers outside.

"It looks like no one has attacked this place," Jake said, looking around at the people there. A few of them looked at him cautiously, but those were mostly the ones who didn't know him.

Kevin nodded. "I guess Pietre is more interested in hitting easy targets right now."

"Why?" Maisy asked. "What's going on?"

"Pietre is trying to create more vampires," Kevin explained, sitting down. "He's obviously scared of something, he was talking about something the hugtandalfers control that might be able to destroy vampires."

"Does Briony know what it is?" Maisy asked.

"She's on the other side again, in Palisor." Kevin hesitated. "With Josh."

Maisy reached out to put a hand over his. She obviously knew how much it hurt for him to be so far away from Briony. But this wasn't about his feelings. They had to focus on getting Briony back, on stopping what was happening in Wicked, and on dealing with Pietre. That was why Kevin reached into his back pocket, searching for something he'd found while going through the werewolves' old things. It had seemed older than the rest. Stranger. He just hoped it had survived all the transformations he'd gone through since.

It was a piece of parchment, which he unfolded carefully, putting it down on the table between them. There were lines scratched on it, coming off a central stave.

"What's this?" Maisy asked.

"I was hoping you could tell me," Kevin said. "I was looking through the werewolves' records, looking for clues, and this is obviously the oldest thing there. I can't read it though."

"This really is old," Maisy said.

"Well," Jake said, coming over to join them, "Josh's family go back to the original werewolves, so that makes a kind of sense."

"Is there any way you can translate it?" Kevin asked.

"Maybe," Steve said, pulling out a laptop from under the table. "I mean, there are translation programs for most things, even languages you wouldn't believe. The only problem is if this is a language nobody on Earth has ever spoken, like one that's exclusive to Palisor?"

"Palisor and this world are linked," Maisy pointed out. "And Archer was able to talk to us, so why would there be languages no one could read?" She started to look over the fragment of parchment.

"Could they be some kind of hieroglyphics?" Kevin asked.

"They look more like Oggam to me," Maisy said. "That's like the closest thing to a written form most of the old celtic languages, like gaelic, had. Try that, Steve."

Steve did, though the two of them argued over a few of the letters as they went, gradually putting it into Steve's computer and letting that work out a translation.

"Right," Maisy said. "It's not exact, because I don't think that the language is quite the same, and anyway, the people who make these programs don't seem to have had vampires and werewolves in mind…"

"But?" Kevin prompted.

"Well, it probably says something like 'when vampires were first made, they were filled with so much evilness that they sought to rule the world, dominate all, and make all those not vampires into slaves or food. Then the werewolves emerged to fight them, to be a guardian against the vampires of the dark. First, the werewolves fought against them over prey, but when they discovered the world of Palisor, stumbling through a…' well, it has to be the gateway, doesn't it '…they gained power. The people there sought werewolves as guards and companions. The most powerful of the werewolves was always the consort of whoever took the crown, and the blending of their powers created a force that drove the vampires from Palisor, destroying those who did not flee."

"That would explain why Pietre was worried," Steve said.

"But I'm not sure it helps us," Kevin replied, shaking his head. "I was hoping for something that would tell me how to get back into Palisor without a dragon."

Steve looked puzzled. "I thought shifters could go through?"

"Only one at a time," Kevin said.

"Like kids in a store?" Maisy said. "But that's…"

"I guess werewolves are too powerful," Kevin said. "That, or maybe even the hugtandalfer are worried about what would happen if the thing that could destroy the vampires were unleashed. Take another look at the fragment I got from Josh's place. Is there anything about getting around the restriction?"

Kailin Gow

Steve shook his head. "There's just what Maisy read out."

"So I can't get in?"

"Not unless you could get Josh to come out," Maisy suggested.

Kevin nodded. "You're right. But what could get Josh to come out of Palisor willingly? What would make him give up everything there? Give up Briony?"

"His kingdom," Jake said. "You know how much Josh likes being in charge here."

Kevin took a deep breath as an idea hit him. "You're right. He's always so careful about reminding people that he's in charge. Even when he left me here, he made such an effort to say that I was only filling in. If he thought I was taking over here, then he'd *have* to come back to try to reassert his claim."

"And try to kick your ass," Jake pointed out.

Kevin shrugged. "He could try. Right now, I'd like a chance to get my hands on him. He tricked all of us."

"So how are you going to take his kingdom off him?" Maisy asked.

"Well, for a start, I'm going to declare myself king," Kevin said. "The first of a whole new line of werewolves. He'll hate that when he hears about it."

"If he hears about it," Steve pointed out. "He's on the other side of the gate, remember?"

Kevin shrugged. "They found out about Briony even while they were over there. They can see here a lot easier than we can see there."

"Okay," Maisy said, "maybe he'd find out. But why would the werewolves accept you. I mean, I know you're alpha, but can you just declare that you're their king? Don't you have to have royal blood, or something?"

"Or he could marry into royalty," Jake said, with a thoughtful expression.

Maisy and Steve both looked at him, smiling as they obviously caught on to whatever idea Briony's brother was having. It took Kevin a moment longer.

"What are you three… on no. *No*. I am *not* marrying Carol."

"But it's the perfect solution," Jake insisted.

"Perfect for whom?" Kevin demanded.

"Well, for all the vampires who aren't a threat to humans," Maisy pointed out. "I mean, if there's genuinely something out there that can destroy all vampires, do you want it here? It could kill Jake."

"Even so…"

"And he's protective of his sister," Jake added. "That alone might be enough to get him to come back here."

"It would be if I were going to marry her," Kevin said. "But I'm not. Do you think I'd betray Briony like that?"

"You'd be doing this *for* Briony," Maisy said. "You heard what we translated. Josh is probably in Palisor even now, trying to find a way to get her to marry him."

Kevin shook his head. "Briony would never do that. She wouldn't agree to marry him."

"She might if it would save her entire kingdom," Steve said.

"And maybe she won't get much of a choice," Maisy added. "You did history at school, right? Princesses never got a lot of say in who they married. If it's like that with the hugtandalfer…"

"Then it could already be too late," Steve finished for her. "And it isn't like you'd actually need to *marry* Carol. Just kind of announce the engagement, at least enough that Josh will believe it and come back."

"It would have to be a long engagement," Kevin said, shaking his head as he said it. Was he really considering this?

"It would have to be a *short* engagement," Maisy countered. "Josh won't come back if he doesn't think there's an immediate threat."

Kevin thought about that for a moment or two, trying to think of a way around it, but he knew that Maisy was right. It was only when he was married that he would be in a position to declare himself the werewolves' king officially, and it was only the threat of that which would bring Josh back.

"Okay," he said at last. "I'll do it. But this is *strictly* pretend. There is no *way* I'd actually do something like this. It would hurt Briony too much."

Chapter 6

Briony looked over at Josh and said the only thing she could think of. "I need time to think about all this."

"Every moment you waste is a moment when there are still vampires in the world," Josh pointed out.

"And I need time to decide what I want to do about that," Briony replied. "Don't try to pressure me any more than you have Josh. You've done enough."

Josh nodded, almost to himself. "I hope so."

Sophie stepped over to him and Fallon. "I think that for now, boys, my niece would like some time alone. Come on, I don't know about you, but I want to get to know the layout of the Cloud Palace."

Josh started to shake his head. "I don't…"

"It wasn't a suggestion," Sophie said, her hand clamping down on his forearm. The three of them left. Briony guessed that her great aunt was planning to have a talk with the two of them, but right then, she couldn't think of anything Sophie could say that might change anything. Josh knew what he wanted, and he'd put her in a position where she didn't have many choices. As far as she knew, he was right. Without the full power of the scepter, she wouldn't be able to control the gates enough to either leave or bring Kevin into Palisor. Not that she knew that much about the gates, even then. They were just things that had been in the way when she'd been trying to get Sophie back or get back home.

But she could think of someone who probably knew a lot more.

Briony found Archer in an enclosed courtyard garden, with climbing flowers covering the walls and sunlight streaming down between the towers of the palace to reflect off a deep pool set in the middle. The dragon was in his human form, that of a gently, almost mischievously good looking boy around her age with white blond hair and golden tanned skin. Today, he wore a white tunic decorated with designs picked out in gold, which seemed to ripple as he turned to her.

"Briony, there you are. You're just in time."

"In time for what? Archer, I wanted to talk to you."

But Archer put his finger to his lips then and pointed to the pool. He might be the dragon bound to her, but that didn't always mean he did what she told him. On the other hand, so far, he'd always done what was in her best interests, so Briony went along with it for the moment, staying quiet and staring at the limpid water.

It didn't stay still and clear for long. Instead, it shifted, ripples appearing on the surface, joining together and shifting until they became images. Briony wasn't sure what she was looking at until she caught sight of Pietre, the master vampire's features utterly unmistakable there in the water.

"It's showing us Wicked?" Briony asked.

"Yes." Archer nodded to the water. "It shows us snatches of what is happening there, or anywhere else."

Briony kept watching for a moment or two while Pietre stood in front of a group of other vampires. They were busy feeding on people they'd dragged into an alley. No, Briony realized, not just feeding on them, because they were giving their victims blood as well as taking it. They were transforming them openly, in the middle of Wicked.

Briony clenched her fists at that sight. She could feel anger bubbling up inside her. Anger and frustration, because there wasn't anything she could do to stop Pietre from here in Palisor. Though that wasn't true, was it? She could stop him right now, if she only married Josh. But then Fallon would die. The thought of that choice made her feel sick.

"Why are you showing me this, Archer?" she asked. "Are you trying to get me to marry Josh?"

Archer shrugged. "That's your choice to make, not mine. I'm your dragon. Whatever you decide, that doesn't change. I just thought you'd want to see Wicked again. This..." Archer gestured to where the vampires were bringing in another citizen of Wicked, and another. "This is just what's happening there."

"But what's happening there is that Pietre's going berserk," Briony said. Then she shook her head. "No, it's worse than that, because that would just be mindless. This... it's like he has some kind of plan. It's systematic, and he's worse than ever. I thought, after everything that had happened with Marcus, and Sophie..."

Archer shrugged. "Someone like Pietre doesn't change easily."

"But he's changing plenty of people," Briony said. "We can't let him do that, Archer. He can't keep changing people into vampires. Where is the Preservation Society?"

The pool shifted briefly, showing an image of people crammed into George's Diner.

"I guess they're doing what they can," Archer said, "but they aren't as strong as the vampires. Kevin is there, with the werewolves, leading them. Maybe they can do something before the vampires get to the gate."

"The gate keeps vampires out," Briony pointed out. "That's what it's there for."

"It might," Archer said. "Then again, it might not."

Briony stared at him. "What are you saying, Archer?"

"The gate is… unstable." Archer paused. "I can't think of a better way to say it. It comes and goes, and I can feel the weakness there. Your father's prohibition against the werewolves seems to be intact, but the rest of it… I think maybe the vampires could come through if they wanted."

"Is there anything we can do about that?" Briony asked, and then saw the look on Archer's face. "Let me guess. If I marry Josh, I'll have the power?"

Archer spread his hands. "Sorry. I know it isn't what you want to hear. I mean, it isn't certain, but the prophecy…"

"I'm starting to hate that prophecy," Briony said with feeling.

Archer nodded. "I'd kind of guessed that. I could be wrong though. We all could. The truth is, no one really knows what's happening. We haven't seen this before. Everything could be different than the way we think. Anyone who tells you that they know exactly what you need to do next is a liar."

Meaning that once again, it was all up to her. Briony didn't know if that was comforting or not. On the one hand, she still had to make her own choices about what happened next, but on the other, there were still all the vague hints that making the wrong one would cut her off from the power she needed to help Palisor.

"What I don't get," Briony said after a minute or so, "is why Pietre is doing this now? Why is he suddenly so desperate to produce new vampires? I mean, he could have done this at any point in the last couple of hundred years. Is it just the gate, or is it something else, because he didn't do this when the gate first showed up."

The picture in the pool changed again, taking them back to Pietre, who was feeding on a young woman now. Briony tried not to think about the fact that she was her age, blonde, and blue eyed. Or about how cruelly painful Pietre was making the feeding.

"My guess is that he knows about the true power the scepter controls," Archer said. "Now that you have it, he must know that it's only a matter of time before that is unleashed and the vampires are wiped out."

Briony thought of Fallon and shuddered slightly. Only a matter of time. Archer made it sound like the deaths of Fallon, Jake, George and every other good vampire were inevitable. Briony couldn't accept that. She *wouldn't* accept that.

"Is it really like the apocalypse for vampires, Archer? All vampires?"

Archer nodded. "That's what they say."

"But how would that happen?" Briony asked. "I mean, are we talking about some kind of magical field of destruction here? Some kind of plague that only kills them?"

"You don't know?" Archer replied, sounding slightly surprised.

"No, of course I don't know. I'm just the princess here. It's not like people actually tell me things. Mostly, I get the feeling that they either think I should know already, like you, or they want to keep things from me to control me, like Josh."

"It's not that," Archer said. "You genuinely don't know? I thought everyone in Palisor knew."

"I'm not *from* Palisor," Briony reminded him. "So just tell me, Archer. What is it? Is it something we can stop, or control?"

Archer shook his head. "I don't think there's much of a chance of that. It isn't really a *thing* at all. It's more of a *who*."

"So who then?" Briony sat down beside the pool, waiting for an answer.

"The greatest slayer there ever was," Archer said. "Him and his army."

"So we'd have a whole army here if I were to marry Josh?" Briony felt her determination not to do that strengthening in that moment. She wasn't going to let something like that happen. She was almost glad in that moment that it was Josh who had crossed over in that moment. That it was Josh the scepter had latched onto as her possible consort. It made it easy to say no. A lot easier than it would have been if it had been Kevin there. With him there, the temptation would have been there to do it. To take him as her consort and just try to deal with the consequences.

Maybe it was the thought of Kevin that made the pool shift again. It certainly seemed to have been shifting with her thoughts and mood so far. Kevin appeared in the pool, in a space Briony recognized as the front lawn of the werewolves' home. His clothing was in tatters, like he'd just transformed from wolf form three or four times in quick succession, displaying his hard muscles and tanned skin underneath. Briony watched him closely, her eyes on his every movement, aching for him as she watched.

Then she saw Carol. Carol's clothing was, if anything, in a worse state than Kevin's. It was barely covering her, though the werewolf didn't seem to care about that at all, in fact, she seemed to be almost flaunting that fact, smiling at Kevin as he got closer to her and shifting so that there were tantalizing glimpses of skin showing along with her curves.

Kevin said something to her, his mouth opening and closing in silent words. It seemed that the pool didn't give them sound. Whatever it was though, it certainly seemed to excite Carol. She threw herself forward at Kevin, flinging her arms around his neck and pulling Kevin close for a kiss that went on for several seconds. It was all Briony could do to keep from jumping into the pond.

"Oh no you don't. You are *not* stealing him."

Archer stared at her, and Briony realized just how forcefully she'd said that.

"Briony? What are you planning to do?"

Briony barely had to think before she had an answer for that one. "I want you in your dragon form, Archer. Now. You're going to take me back through that gate, whatever it takes, and then… then I'm going to go get Kevin back. *She* is not having him."

Chapter 7

Kevin headed over to the werewolves' mansion in his wolf form. It was the quickest way to cover the distance, and he wanted to get this over with. He still wasn't quite sure how he'd let Jake and the others talk him into this. Except that he was going to do this. Briony. Unless he did this, he might never get to see her again, and he couldn't risk that.

He changed back on the lawn in front of the majestic house, which was neatly maintained in spite of being in the middle of a forest. The mansion itself was whitewashed and looked like the kind of place that might have been preserved as a monument from centuries ago, but very carefully. There were no traces of dilapidation around the werewolves' house.

As Kevin stood there, he was only too aware of the fact that he'd changed plenty of times in the same clothes. They hung off him now, rumpled and torn by the forces that came into play during the transformation. With most people, he would have worried about meeting them like this because of what they would have thought. With Carol, who had seen plenty of other werewolves like this, that wouldn't be a problem, but there might be other difficulties if she took it as an invitation.

The problem with Carol was... well, actually, there wasn't a problem. Maybe *that* was the problem. She was pretty, closer to his age than Briony was, not to mention a werewolf just like him. And she was obviously interested in him. She'd made that clear plenty of times. Under other circumstances, Kevin could easily have seen himself getting together with her. Though maybe not for long. There were a few things about her that were more of a worry, like the fact that she didn't seem to care too much for humans, and like that temper of hers. Even those had explanations though.

Kevin found himself thinking about Carol's temper then. How would she react to the idea of just pretending to be engaged? It wasn't so much a question of whether she'd be angry as simply *how* angry she'd be. Yet with Briony at stake, Kevin decided that he didn't care. He could deal with Carol's anger.

The sleek shape of a she wolf padded onto the lawn, looking up at him with intense eyes. Carol transformed then, her hair falling in wild tangles as she shot up into her human form. It wasn't the only thing wild about her. Her clothing was in complete disarray, torn now from her transformations in a way it hadn't been in town. It barely covered her.

Carol seemed to know it, too. She shifted provocatively, seeming to enjoy Kevin's eyes on her as glimpses of her flesh shifted beneath the cloth.

"Like what you see, Kevin?" Carol laughed as she said it, reaching out a hand to trace down Kevin's chest through his shirt. "I know I do."

"Carol," Kevin said. "I need to talk to you. It's important."

"It sounds serious," Carol said. She rolled her eyes. "Not more vampires."

Kevin shook his head, trying to stop himself from pulling back. It wouldn't exactly work, asking Carol to be his fiancé while shying away from even her touch.

"No, it's not that, but it is serious," he said. He tried to work out how much to tell her. Would she go along with it if he explained everything? Would she agree to simply pretend? The truth was that she had no reason to pretend. Especially not when it meant tricking her brother. Which meant that Kevin couldn't afford to explain all the details, even though that would end up hurting her later on. Was he okay with that?

"I hope this isn't going to be all about *Briony*, then," Carol said. "Because these days, it seems like it's always either vampires or her." She rearranged her clothing again, but not to cover her any better. "I bet we could think of better things to talk about than your ex if we wanted."

Yes, Kevin decided, he was absolutely fine with it.

"Actually," he said, "I wanted to talk about us."

"Us?" That seemed to make Carol pause. "I didn't think there *was* an us. I mean…" she bit her lip. "I didn't think you noticed me."

"It's pretty hard not to," Kevin said, absolutely truthfully. "And with Briony not here, I've been thinking about you a lot more recently. That, and I've been thinking about what you said before, about me being nearly a king.

I've been thinking about that a lot. And I can't deny that there's something between us. I think it's something big."

Carol looked up at him carefully. "What are you saying, Kevin?"

"I'm saying..." Kevin took a breath, steeling himself to force the words out. "Carol, will you marry me?"

The kiss caught him by surprise. Carol threw her arms around his neck, but didn't move up on tiptoes to kiss him. Instead, she pulled him down to her level to kiss him, her mouth rough, almost fierce, against his. Her hands tangled in his hair almost painfully, and Carol seemed to enjoy the small sound of protest he made, at least if the way she kept kissing him was anything to go by. Her tongue started to explore his mouth hungrily.

Kevin had to admit that there was something about being this close to a powerful, aggressive woman like this. One who knew what she wanted and wasn't afraid to take it. It was something that was surprisingly attractive, and Kevin could feel himself responding when Carol's hands started to drift lower than his chest.

"Of course," Carol whispered to him, her voice husky, "once you become the king, you'll need someone to show you the ropes. Someone to guide you. I hope you're prepared to listen when a woman tells you what to do, Kevin."

But there was still Briony to consider. Whatever Carol made him feel, it wasn't even close to the way he felt every time he was around Briony. It wasn't the same. Which was why Kevin pulled back as Carol moved to continue her seduction.

"No," he said, "I can't."

Carol raised an eyebrow. "No? You aren't feeling shy, are you?"

"It's not that. It's…"

"It's the fact that you're using me to try to manipulate my brother?" Carol smiled, and then suddenly her leg was hooked around Kevin's, so that when she shoved him, he went stumbling to the floor. Carol followed him, kneeling above him. Her fingers traced over his chest again, only this time her nails dug in hard enough to make Kevin wince. "Did you think I was stupid, Kevin?"

"What?" Actually, there had been part of him that had thought it wouldn't be a problem to trick her. Carol had always been so impulsive, and Kevin had been banking on her going along with another decision without thinking too hard.

She slapped him then. Not hard, but not playfully, either. Above him, her features contorted into a brief expression of anger. "That's for trying to manipulate me, for not paying attention, and for thinking the way all stupid male werewolves seem to."

"Carol..."

"Shh!" She put a finger to his lips, and a playful edge seemed to return to her. "You're going to have to learn not to interrupt. Another thing that you men never seem to get the hang of. Take my brothers. Brian was always talking over me, and Josh... he always assumed that since he was the clever one and I was just a girl, I had to be stupid. You've heard the way he talks to me."

Kevin had, though as he remembered it, Carol was mostly trying to persuade him to hurt Briony at the time. That or coming up with ideas that had more to do with her anger than anything else.

"All of you men seem to be the same," Carol said. "You see a werewolf girl like me and you try to treat me like something out of the nineteenth century. Like I don't *matter*, and like I can't possibly come up with an idea that might be worthwhile."

"What about Channing?" Kevin asked. "He didn't treat you like that."

That got a wince of pain from Carol. "Channing was better than the rest of them. He understood. He…" she shook her head. "But he's gone now, and we aren't going to talk about him."

"Then what are we going to talk about?" Kevin asked. He wondered if he could roll Carol off him. She was smaller and lighter than him, but she knew enough about fighting that it would be hard to do.

She leaned down and kissed him again then. This kiss was softer and gentler than the first one had been, but it was no less controlling. Kevin jerked his head away, risking the possibility of another slap, but Carol didn't seem bothered. If anything, she smiled.

"I like that. You aren't some weakling who's going to give up just like that. You're worthy of me, Kevin. You're the only man around here who is. But even you… I won't let you control me and manipulate me like that. I won't let you *use* me like that. Which is why it's probably a good thing that I'm the one with all the cards here."

"Are you going to let me up?" Kevin asked.

"Why, when I have you where I want you?" Carol shuffled a little higher on his chest and pinned his arms. "In every sense."

"So what do you want?" Kevin asked. Carol was obviously enjoying this. Far too much for his liking. Yet what could he do about it? Besides, she was right. He had tried to manipulate her.

"Haven't you been paying attention?" Carol asked. "I want all those big bad wolves in our pack to have to do what I tell them. I want them to stop ignoring me. I want them to get down on their knees the way they so obviously want to every time they look at you. And for that, I'm going to need you."

"How?" Kevin asked.

"Exactly the way you already offered." Carol slid off him then, moving to lay beside him on the grass, propped up on one elbow, so that to anyone watching they would have looked like a happy couple enjoying the sun. "We're going to get married, Kevin. And before you start complaining, remember that you suggested it first. You're getting what you wanted."

She reached out to stroke his face. "And I want you to know that I *do* want you. If I'd thought that you'd give yourself to me willingly… that you actually cared about me rather than *her*… I just want you to know that, so you don't think it's all about the power."

"What power?" Kevin demanded. "It sounds like you're offering to make me the werewolves' king."

"There you go thinking like a man again," Carol said. "Deciding that you must be more important. You're a *bitten* wolf. You're a powerful enough alpha to make a play for the throne, but *I'm* the one who was born a werewolf. You wouldn't be king, Kevin. You'd just be a consort."

"And you?"

Carol smiled. "I have no parents. Two of my brothers are dead, and the one who's left is too busy playing around in other worlds to look after his people. I think the werewolves need a new queen."

Chapter 8

Briony headed back to her room with Archer in tow, practically running through the palace in search of a good place to leave from. In her room, she checked that the head of the scepter was safely stowed around her neck, and then started to hunt through the room's furniture in search of her old clothes. There was no sign of them though.

"It looks like I'm going to have to go home like this," she said aloud, trying not to think about how she'd look walking down the main street of Wicked dressed like something out of a Renaissance Faire. Then she looked at Archer and smiled. Somehow, she suspected that flying in on a dragon would make people stare a little more than the dress.

"Come on Archer, let's get going."

She strode over to the open window and the balcony beyond. It would be easy for him to transform there, and then... then they would be on their way, looking for a gate to take them back. Briony didn't have full control over them yet, so they'd have to find one, but if anyone could find a route back to Wicked, Archer could.

"Briony? What are you doing?"

Briony turned to see Fallon coming back into the room. He was staring at her like he knew that something was wrong. Maybe he did. "I thought Sophie was giving you and Josh the tour."

"She was. I slipped away to see you." He moved forward to catch hold of her elbow. "What's going on, Briony?"

"I have to go back to Wicked," she explained. "I saw it in one of the reflecting pools they have here. Pietre is transforming people, and I can't allow that."

What she didn't say was that she couldn't stay there when that would mean marrying Josh. When it would mean unleashing whoever it was who would kill all the vampires, including Fallon, Jake and George. It was easier to think about the need to protect the people of Wicked, and to concentrate on the way she was meant to be heading up the Preservation Society. She couldn't do that in Palisor.

She couldn't see Kevin again here either. Josh had been wrong about that part. She didn't have to marry him to see Kevin again. She just had to go back. Though that… she thought about the sight of Carol and Kevin kissing. Just the memory of the image hurt. How could Kevin have done that? With *her*?

Was this how he felt every time she kissed Fallon? How Fallon felt when she was with Kevin?

There was one other reason she wanted to go back then. She wanted Pietre gone. It wasn't enough to just keep protecting people from him anymore. He wasn't going to stop until he was killed. And if Briony wasn't prepared to unleash the end of the vampires to do that, if she couldn't bear to lose the others who would be killed, then that meant she owed it to the world to finish Pietre off herself.

Fallon looked into her eyes, and in that moment, Briony knew that he'd guessed exactly what she had planned. She couldn't keep anything hidden from him, not then. "You're not planning to take on Pietre alone? No, you can't. Not like that."

"I have to."

"Well, you aren't doing it alone," Fallon insisted. "I'm coming with you. I'd go to the ends of the earth for you. I can definitely go back to Wicked."

"Fallon…"

Fallon kissed her then. He pulled Briony to him sharply and kissed her passionately, holding her against him while he did it. He didn't seem to care that Archer was there, or that someone might walk in and see them. He didn't seem to care about anything but her. He pulled back, still staring into her eyes. Once, that might have caught her, entranced her, just through the power that vampires had. Now, there was nothing holding Briony there but how beautiful Fallon was. That was enough though.

"I know the feeling that you're getting from the scepter. I know that everyone thinks that it has somehow chosen you to be with Josh, but that doesn't matter to me. All that matters is what you want. What's in your heart, Briony?"

Briony stalled, trying to think. The truth was that she didn't know what was in her heart. If she did, her life would be a lot simpler than it was. She did know who *wasn't* in her heart though.

"Are you saying that I should just ignore what the people of my kingdom want?"

"Yes," Fallon said, simply. "If it isn't what you want. It *isn't* what you want, is it?"

Briony shook her head. "No. It's not just Josh. I can't marry him when it would mean the deaths of all vampires. It would kill Jake, George…"

"Me."

"Yes," Briony said, and then Fallon kissed her again. This kiss was softer, sweeter.

"You still care about me then?" Fallon asked.

"You know I do."

"It's hard to tell, sometimes. But you… you're the only girl I've ever loved, Briony. I've never wanted anyone else. And it's more than that. You're the reason I manage to stop myself from hurting people. You're my reason for staying good. Every time it feels like the hunger might be stronger than me, I think about how you'd look if you knew. I think about how much it would hurt you."

"It shouldn't be about me," Briony said. She wasn't comfortable with Fallon putting that much on her, because what would it mean if she didn't end up with him. "You should do the right thing *because* it's the right thing, not because of me."

Fallon shook his head. "But it isn't about that for us, Briony. Look at George. He's stayed good because of how much he loves Sophie. Jake… he loves you and Sophie. Every vampire I've heard of who doesn't feed on humans manages it because they love someone. It's like that love reminds us what it's like to be human. It's that love that makes the difference."

"I love you too, Fallon," Briony said, because that was true. No matter how complicated everything else got, that would always be true.

Their third kiss was as passionate as any they'd ever had, their hands roaming over one another as they kissed deeply, ignoring Archer's presence in the background completely. Briony felt the moment when Fallon's fangs appeared, but that was okay, because hers were there in the same moment. They stood back, looking at one another and then laughing.

"We need to go," Briony said.

Fallon nodded. "Both of us?"

"Both of us. Archer?"

Archer stepped out onto the palace balcony, hopping up onto the rail as lightly as an acrobat. He shifted then, and the difference seemed impossible, the way it always did. One moment there was just a good looking boy their age standing there, the next...

His dragon form didn't make the balcony creak, but that just suggested that it had been reinforced to withstand it. The giant, golden form of the dragon perched there like some great bird, Archer's wings spread out so that they caught the light and shone. Briony clambered up onto his back easily, while Fallon climbed up behind her, wrapping his arms around her. Briony liked that. So often, it seemed to be her relying on him.

Archer leapt into the air, and for a second he hung there, giving Briony a perfect view out over the waterfall beneath, with the rainbows hanging in the falling flow. Then he dropped along it, plunging down through the billowing cloud while Briony clung to him and Fallon clung to her, his wings pulled back tight.

They spread again, and Archer leveled out, taking them out over a panorama of fields and forest so far below that they seemed somehow unreal, like a patchwork quilt or some kind of child's drawing.

"Find a gate for us, Archer," Briony said. "Get us back to Wicked."

Archer roared his assent and wheeled, obviously scanning the ground below. He seemed to find what he was looking for, because he picked out a line of flight and set off along it, a swooping golden arrow through the air. He took them lower now, low enough that they could make out occasional figures in the fields and pick out the details of scattered houses, where hugtandalfer lived and worked. Briony saw creatures below too, winged griffons flying closer to the ground, a giant tall enough that he dwarfed the trees beside him.

Then she saw something that gleamed golden in the sunlight, as bright as Archer's scales were. It seemed like a simple beam of light, or maybe the reflection of something below, down in the middle of a stretch of woodland below.

"What's that?" Briony asked, pointing.

Fallon followed the direction of her pointing finger. "I'm not sure. It looks like something in the woods, reflecting. Here, it could be anything."

That was true, and Briony was about to let Archer fly past it when she felt the tingling of the scepter head. It lay against her chest, worn around her neck like a pendant, and the metal of it was suddenly warm against her skin.

"The scepter is doing something," Briony said. "I... I think it might have something to do with whatever's below."

Archer circled the spot where the gleam had come from, flapping his leathery wings in slow, graceful movements, almost hanging in the air. While he did that, Briony tried to pay more attention to the head of the scepter, trying to work out why it would respond like that and what there was about whatever was below that was so important. She still didn't understand everything about how the scepter worked; she just knew that it was a repository for the power of royal hugtandalfer, and so had the essence of generations of her ancestors within it. Did that mean it also had something of their personalities locked away inside it? The truth was that Briony didn't know, yet in things like its reaction to Josh and the way it had responded to her, it sometimes felt almost like the scepter had a life of its own.

Which was why she wasn't surprised when she suddenly knew, simply *knew* that she needed to investigate what lay below. That it was important, and it was for her. She didn't know how she knew it, but she knew it nonetheless. It was like something she'd half-forgotten and just remembered, except that the memory had never been hers in the first place.

"We need to go down," Briony said. "I don't know what's down there, but the scepter is responding to it so strongly…"

Even as she said that, the scepter started to vibrate more, so that it thrummed against her skin.

"We need to go down *now*," Briony repeated. "Whatever that golden glow is, I get the feeling that… that it's for me."

Archer was obviously paying attention, despite the rush of wind past them. His circling turned into a spiral, and with each sweeping pass he went lower, heading for a break in the trees. Whatever was down there, it seemed that the dragon agreed. They needed to find out what it was.

Chapter 9

Archer flew down, still circling, heading for the open space where they'd seen the golden glow, and towards which the scepter seemed to be pulling Briony. Looking down, she could see that the area below was rocky, the stone hard enough that the trees couldn't grow up over it. It was also higher up than most of the land around it, the trees having disguised the contours of the land from the air so that it was only as they landed that Briony realized they were on the highest point of land for several miles.

Mist seemed to curl between the trees as they got lower, and Briony suspected that couldn't be natural. Though with Palisor, it was impossible to know for certain. Maybe that slope accounted for the roughness of Archer's landing, because the jolt of it was enough to tumble Fallon out from behind her, while even Briony found herself sliding down the dragon's scales to land flat footed on the rocks beneath. She managed to stop herself from stumbling, which wasn't easy in the long dress, but she managed it.

"Sorry," Archer said, and when Briony turned he was in his golden haired human form again.

By that point though, Briony wasn't listening, because the scepter was pulling her towards the tree line. Literally pulling her, because right then it felt like the thing might either yank off the chain that held it around her neck or physically drag her forward, so that the only way to avoid being choked by it was to go in the direction of the pull.

There was a path there, a narrow track that looked like it had been formed by the passage of animals through the woods. There were even hoof prints there, though Briony couldn't work out the kind of animal that they were from. Maybe some kind of horse? She didn't have the time to stop and check with the others though, because the scepter was still pulling her on, so that she had to walk quickly to keep up.

The hem of her pale dress was quickly crusted with mud, and at least once it snagged on branches, because the path didn't seem very clear. It was like no one had walked along it for a while. No one human, at least. Briony saw a tuft of white hair caught on a branch ahead, clearly from some kind of animal. With Fallon and Archer following in her wake, she sped up as she walked along the path.

The trees around them started to change, their leaves turning silvery as the three of them continued along the path. Soon, it was as though they were walking between two curtains of shimmering precious metal, the scepter still firmly indicating that it was this way Briony had to go.

Ahead, the silver branches parted, moving aside as Briony stepped towards them, revealing another expanse of bare stone. A kind of natural stone table, little more than a rough block of granite worn by the weather, sat a little way away, while beside it…

It was a unicorn. There was no other word for it. It was a horse higher at the shoulder than Briony was tall, with a hide so white that it seemed almost to glow from within. Its eyes were the same silver as the leaves on the trees, and there was a horn jutting from the center of its forehead, golden and gleaming. Briony had glimpsed unicorns from the air before, flying over them with Archer, but this one was somehow different.

Kailin Gow

"It's the sacred unicorn," Archer said, and the dragon sounded like he was in awe. "Look at it."

"What's so special about it?" Fallon asked, and Briony found herself wondering how he couldn't see that *everything* about it was special.

"They say it was the first creature in Palisor," Archer whispered, just behind Briony. "They say that its horn contains more magic than all the kings of Palisor put together. I never thought I'd see it."

It seemed odd to Briony that they would suddenly find a creature this powerful, unless…

"Is this what Pietre was afraid of?" she asked.

Archer shook his head. "This isn't the slayer. The unicorn doesn't have an army. It doesn't need one."

"Then how did we find it?" Briony continued to look at the creature as she asked that. It seemed like too much of a coincidence. Even with the scepter showing them the way, why had they spotted it now?

"You found me because I wished to be found." The words were clear, deep and strong. They sounded even though the lips of the unicorn didn't move. The voice of the creature was male and gently authoritative; a voice to be obeyed out of love, not fear. "You found me because Palisor and your world do not need the slaying army now. That could be worse than the threat it is set free to counter. You need another way, and I have that, though the price is a great one."

Briony turned her head slightly, looking to Archer for guidance. The dragon shrugged.

"I don't know what you should do, Briony. Isn't the scepter telling you anything? You should trust that."

"Ah, the scepter," the unicorn said. "You carry it, and the blood of royalty. Two parts of a prophecy, but also the way to many other things. You are the only one of the direct line left now, aren't you? You are the Queen?"

Briony nodded. "Yes. I am."

"Then I was right. It's time. You must do what is needed to make sure that my land stays safe from harm."

Its land. Maybe Archer was right about it being the first creature in Palisor.

"What do I have to do?" Briony asked. She remembered something the creature had said before. "You said something about there being a price. What price?"

The unicorn tilted its head towards a stone table. On it, now that she could take her eyes off the unicorn long enough to look, Briony could see a knife of purest obsidian, the handle made from the same granite as the table.

"The price is mine to pay," the unicorn said, "but it will not be easy for you either. You must slay me, Briony, Queen of Palisor. You must take the knife, take my life, and take my horn. My horn shall be your weapon against the vampires. It will give you the power to be the greatest slayer of their kind who has lived. It will give you a way to do what you must do to protect your people."

Briony tried to stall, asking the obvious question. "I thought I had to marry Josh. The scepter chose him. Why would it lead me to you if it chose him?"

"This 'Josh' is a werewolf?" the unicorn asked.

Briony nodded.

"Then it would have singled him out according to the temperature of his blood. Vampires are cool in their death. Werewolves run hot. They are opposites. The scepter has enough of the power of the dead kings in it to sense that, and to sense that a powerful werewolf would be enough to stand beside you."

"So it's an accident?" Briony asked. "It could have been any werewolf? But why didn't I feel that with Kevin? He's… um… another werewolf."

"One you like better than this 'Josh'." It wasn't a question. "Did you stand in Palisor with this other werewolf while you held the scepter?"

Briony tried to think, and then shook her head. "No. I don't think so."

"Then that is the difference."

"So I have a choice about who I marry?"

"Of course you do," the unicorn said. "I'm doing this largely so that you *do* have a choice. Though you should know that even for the full power of my horn to be revealed, you will need to be married to one powerful enough to be worthy of it, whoever that is."

Briony didn't know what to say to that, or what to feel in that moment. There was relief, definitely, that she didn't have to marry Josh. There was a kind of gratitude for what the unicorn was trying to give her, and maybe excitement at the possibility of having something that would make it easier to deal with Pietre. Yet to get all that, she would still have to kill this magnificent, intelligent, powerful creature.

"I don't want to hurt you," Briony said to it.

The unicorn dipped its head. "I know that, and that is part of what makes you worthy to do it. You are not like the first slayer of vampires. You do not kill easily. You protect those around you. If any must take my horn, then I would have it be you. It will bring peace to Palisor and to the Wicked Woods. That is my purpose now, so take the knife, use it, and make me proud."

"I can't," Briony started to say, but she found her hand reaching out for the stone of the dagger. She ran her thumb down the blade without even thinking about it, watching a bead of blood well up almost like it didn't belong to her.

The scepter. The scepter was doing this, because Briony could feel the power of it pulsing through her in a compulsion she wasn't sure that she could fight. And she could feel another power with it, a power that seemed in her mind to glow as golden as the unicorn's horn.

"I'm sorry," the unicorn said, "but I can't let you shy away from this."

Her arm swept out, holding the dagger, which she plunged into the unicorn's heart. It toppled, collapsing onto its side, staring up at her. "I'm so sorry," Briony cried, tears running down her cheeks, as her body was led by the scepter to complete her task. Briony was sure that she felt the moment when it died, something changing in the pull of the scepter, but that didn't stop her from doing what she had to do next, no matter how gruesome it was. She set to work with the knife even while tears fell from her eyes, the compulsion that had made her strike holding her there until the golden shaft of the horn sat in her hand, as smeared with blood as the rest of her.

The unicorn had paid its price. It had given up its life, just like that. Just for her. Briony knelt there, staring at the horn as though seeing it for the first time. She knelt there while Archer and Fallon dragged away the body of the first creature of Palisor. She stared at the horn while they buried it, trying to work out how what she held could possibly be worth what she'd just had to do.

She knew how she had to use it. It was a stake. *The* stake. One that would give her a chance against Pietre and his vampires without having to call up a threat that would kill all of their kind. She forced herself to stand and looked at Archer. She didn't know how her face looked right then, but even the dragon seemed nervous.

"Change back into your dragon form," Briony commanded. "We have a gate home to find."

Chapter 10

They rose up over the clearing again, clinging tightly to Archer's back. The dragon's wings lifted him sharply, leaving the spot where Briony had slain the unicorn behind in a matter of seconds. It couldn't happen quickly enough for her then, though with the golden horn of the beast pushed into her belt and the creature's blood still staining her clothing, some parts of the last few minutes weren't so easy to leave behind.

"Get us to the gate, Archer," Briony ordered and the dragon swooped around, heading in the direction that he had been going before they had found the unicorn. That didn't last for more than a few seconds though because then Archer wheeled around.

"What is it?" Briony asked him, but flying there, with the head of the scepter around her neck, she knew. She could feel it the same way that she'd been able to feel the gate through to here before. The gate that Archer had found was gone, vanished from the face of Palisor in whatever cycle of appearances and disappearances governed them.

"No," Briony said. "No. It *can't* be."

Archer made a huffing sound, and Briony knew that she'd guessed correctly.

"What is it?" Fallon asked her.

"The gate is gone," Briony said. She wasn't going to give up that easily though. "Archer, can you find another?"

The dragon's head looked around at her and the answer was obvious even to Briony, but she couldn't give up that easily. Not when Pietre was on the other side, making more vampires. Not when Kevin was on the other side with... with *her*.

"Try, Archer," she insisted, knowing that because it was her asking the dragon wouldn't be able to refuse. He was her dragon, and he could no more ignore an order from her than give up breathing.

Archer roared his displeasure, but he did as Briony commanded, flying out over fields and streams, broken land and marsh, trying to find a way through into Wicked. Into anywhere in the real world. As far as Briony was concerned, even a portal through into Alaska would work, because at least that would be on the right plane of existence. They could deal with getting back to Wicked from there.

Archer flew on, and on. Behind her, Briony could feel Fallon getting restless.

"How long are we going to keep going?" he asked. "If the gate's gone, then-"

"There will be another gate," Briony insisted. "Somewhere, there will be another gate."

"It took Sophie decades to find a way through," Fallon pointed out. "The gates aren't that simple, Briony. Even with the scepter, they don't just come when you call."

"We keep going," Briony said, and Fallon must have heard the determination in her voice, because he didn't continue to argue. Maybe it was killing the unicorn that had done it. Maybe having to do something so terrible had pushed her over the edge. Or maybe, Briony thought, it was just that, having done that, if they couldn't get into Wicked, it meant that the creature's death was in vain. She couldn't allow that.

So they kept going. Archer flew in circles, completing ever wider circuits with the castle somewhere at their center. He flew over villages and track ways, rolling hills and forest. Briony had never seen so much of her kingdom. They even flew over the darker lands where there was nothing but broken rock, and it seemed like even the sun took on muted shades. She hadn't been there since Marcus' brother had kidnapped her and tried to persuade her to fetch the scepter for him.

Archer swung back around over the kingdom, and Briony could see that the sun was setting there too now. Had they really been flying for so many hours? She could see now that Archer's wings were moving more slowly, and she could hear the great huffs of breath that came with every stroke of them against the air. Even his supernatural strength was starting to wane.

"All right, Archer," Briony said at last, knowing that it was no use. "Go back to the castle. We'll try again tomorrow."

And the next day. And every day after that until they found a way through. It was then that she heard the rumbling. It was low, barely registering with her at first, but it went on, not stopping for several minutes. An earthquake. A big one too, from the sound of the shaking. Yet they were far enough above it that it wasn't a threat, and in any case all the land around them was simply open fields.

"Just keep heading for the castle," Briony urged Archer. They kept flying, eating up the distance slowly now that the dragon was tired, but still going.

A purple and green streak shot past them. Briony turned, recognizing the shape of another dragon. Recognizing the dragon too. It was Fletcher, Archer's brother and the dragon of King Waltham before her father's death. Fletcher wheeled to move alongside them, and then let out a hissing cry that Archer apparently understood, because he started to lose height.

Fletcher landed in an open field. The castle was on the horizon, but Archer didn't seem interested in it. Instead, he landed beside his brother, who was back in his purple haired human form by then. It was that of a lean teenager who looked a lot like Archer, though a little shorter and with a tendency towards much darker clothes. The whole effect was vaguely Goth, though Briony suspected that wasn't deliberate. Briony slid down off Archer's back with Fallon beside her, looking over at the dragon.

"Fletcher, what are you doing here? Why have you brought us down in a field like this?"

"Forgive me, my queen, but it could not wait. There was something I had to check after King Waltham died, and it seems urgent to tell you. You felt the earth shake?"

"An earthquake," Briony said.

"But what caused it?" Fletcher counted.

"I guess the answer isn't going to be 'shifting tectonic plates'," Fallon put in from beside her.

"What are those?" Fletcher shook his head. "No. This came because in the east of your kingdom, a chasm was opening up. One that we had thought long closed. One *held* closed by the power of your father."

"So when he died, it stopped holding it?" Briony asked. It sounded like another thing about this kingdom that no one had told her, and that was now her responsibility. "Why was the chasm closed?"

"It was a place to keep the worst creatures," Fletcher explained. "The ones too dangerous to walk the light."

"Um..." Briony wondered how to put it. "Wasn't *Marcus* too dangerous to be allowed to stay here?"

Fletcher shrugged. "Marcus and his brother were too strong together to deal with. And they were intelligent enough to stop us from destroying them. You might not believe this, but when he killed his brother, Marcus made it a lot easier for you to kill him."

"That was meant to be *easy*?" Briony said.

"Easier than it was before," Archer replied. He was back in his human form now. He looked exhausted. "Fletcher, are you saying that Xylyx is open?"

"Xylyx?" Briony asked. "What's Xylyx?"

"It's the name of the abyss where the most dangerous creatures on Palisor live," Fletcher explained. "This chasm is a way in, and more importantly, it's a way out. Creatures that haven't been seen in Palisor for thousands of years will pour from it if we can't deal with this. Including the Bestial."

"What's that?" Fallon asked.

Fletcher shook his head. "It's more a case of 'who are they?' They're fanged creatures. Some say that they were once hugtandalfer who gave themselves over to evil and were changed by it to become the original vampires. Some say that they simply sprang up as vampires, an original, pure form driven by blood. Whatever they were though, now they are little more than beasts, driven by the need for blood and violence."

"Like Marcus' vampires?" Briony asked.

"Worse. Marcus' vampires were barbaric and savage, but these… they don't speak. They don't plan. They don't take prisoners. They just kill, and kill, until they're stopped. And they might not even be the worst of what's coming out of the chasm."

Briony paused, because she knew what was going to come next. As the Queen of Palisor, she had to deal with it. It was going to be her responsibility. She would have to go out to slay the creatures, or gather armies, or maybe even marry Josh to get the power to deal with them, despite what she'd just gained with the horn taken from the unicorn.

Yet the truth was there was a part of her that just wanted to ignore all of that and keep searching for a way back to Wicked. *That* was her home, even if this was her kingdom. And Kevin… Kevin wasn't in Palisor. He was back in Wicked with Carol, and right then, if it was a straight choice between monsters here and Carol back there with Kevin, Briony knew which one was the greater threat to her.

She squashed those feelings, though. What was important to her wasn't the same thing as what was *important*. If she did run out on her kingdom just to find Kevin, that might be what her heart told her, but it wasn't what was right. She couldn't have the deaths of all the people of her kingdom on her conscience. She might want to go, but she knew she couldn't.

Not that she really had much of a choice in the matter. It wasn't like there was a gate back across now anyway. Right then, it felt almost like the whole kingdom was conspiring to keep her there to protect against this threat. Maybe it was. The scepter could control the gates, and it had the essences of the old kings and queens of her realm within. Maybe it had sensed the threat and shut down the gates to help protect Palisor. Briony guessed that she would never know for certain.

Kailin Gow

"We should act quickly," Archer said. "After so long in captivity, they won't wait before they start to destroy what they can. They'll want revenge."

"The ones that can understand the idea, at least," Fletcher added. "The rest... destruction is just what they are."

Briony made at least one final attempt, because there was more than even Kevin at stake back home. "What about Wicked? Pietre is back there transforming people. I can't just leave them and let him do that."

"You have to," Archer said. "Palisor has to be your priority, and not just because you're its queen. If it falls, then the gates between the worlds will be without protection. The creatures from the chasm will be able to cross with impunity. Then no one will be safe. Not even in Wicked."

Chapter 11

They flew, speeding back towards the Cloud Palace. Archer's exhaustion seemed to be forgotten for the moment, and he powered them back in quick, efficient strokes of his wings. Briony hadn't seen the Cloud Palace properly as she'd left it. She hadn't been looking back, but now she could see it, the elegant spires and rises of the palace seeming to grow out of the rock around it, so that the whole building seemed to be a part of the mountain top it stood on.

They didn't fly back towards the balcony they'd taken off from. Instead, they headed for a flat space on the roof that reminded Briony a little of a helipad. A dragon pad, perhaps? There were figures standing on it, and Briony recognized them with a sinking feeling as Archer took her closer. Sophie was there, and Josh. Prince Vigor, the hugtandalfer man her father had adopted to be his heir if he couldn't get his daughter back, was there too. He was a large, powerfully built hugtandalfer with hair of alternating black and silver stripes, his eyes solid silver and his features possibly the most beautiful of any man Briony had seen. Certainly beautiful enough that Sophie liked him. A lot.

They'd be angry, of course. Her great aunt would be angry that she'd run off without telling her. Josh would be furious that she'd run away from him. And Vigor... he would probably be the angriest of all, that the girl who had taken what could have been his throne would try to run out on her kingdom. Yet right then, there wasn't the time for them to be angry. Not if Fletcher was right.

Briony leapt down from Archer's back, and she could see the way Sophie's face changed as she saw the blood on her.

"Briony, what have you been doing?"

Briony shook her head. "That isn't important. What's important is that Fletcher just told me we might be attacked. There are apparently-"

Vigor held up a hand. "We know about Xylyx." He took something from his belt, and Briony realized that it was an old fashioned brass telescope. He passed it to her, pointing. "We weren't just up here waiting for you. Look there, Princess."

Briony looked in the direction he was indicating, but even so, it took her a moment or two to understand what she was seeing, because for a moment or two, it just looked black. Then she understood. It was darkness and shadow, roiling around like cloud. Briony thought that she could see glimpses of things in it, but they were gone almost as soon as she saw them.

"This should not be happening," Vigor said. "The legends say that as long as the first of us stands, even without the kings, the chasm will stay closed."

"Um…" Briony said. "There might be a problem there."

She explained what had happened with the unicorn. Vigor looked horrified.

"How could you do something like that? Without the throne truly settled, every force in this land will rise to try to take it."

"Well, it's not like you ever told me that," Briony pointed out. "Besides, I thought I was the queen now. I thought it *was* settled."

Vigor smiled a ghost of a smile. "Things are never that easy. Look at the history of kings and queens in your own world. They would have the attributes to take a throne, but they would still have to take it and hold it. You have the scepter, and King Waltham's blood, but you still have to win. The creatures of Xylyx are rising up now because they think there is no one to stop them, and if they win…"

"If they win," Sophie said, "they will destroy us. These aren't Pietre's vampires, who want to control people without being seen. They aren't Marcus', who wanted to enslave people. These will just kill, and kill, until there is nothing left in Palisor. Then they will turn to our world and start the slaughter again."

"Then we can't let them win," Briony said. "But I guess this time it isn't just going to be about us."

Fletcher and Archer stepped forward. Fletcher spoke. "You are right, Your Majesty. Our best hope is for everyone in Palisor to fight. The hugtandalfer and the dragons both."

"Not just them," Sophie put in, looking over the edge of the parapet. "Palisor is full of creatures that have relied on the protection of the hugtandalfer, but it is time for them to fight. They can't just hide and hope that someone else will solve their problems."

Josh hadn't said anything until then, but Briony had been aware of him watching her. She couldn't guess at what he was thinking.

"How big is your army, Vigor?" Josh asked.

"A few thousand now," Vigor replied with a trace of pride. "There wasn't much before, but since the old king's death, I've been recruiting able bodied men and women and training them. We aren't going to be helpless. We can choose not to be helpless."

Briony smiled at the prince. Under his gruff demeanor and his apparent disdain for her before, he was actually a smart, thoughtful man. Not to mention a handsome one. Josh looked from her to Vigor, obviously catching the look.

He snorted. "A few thousand isn't going to be enough. I know how bad Pietre's vampires were, and how bad Marcus' vampires were. If these are worse, then a rabble put together at short notice won't be enough to stop them."

"The hugtandalfer aren't a rabble," Vigor said in a dangerous tone. "If you doubt our ability to fight, I could show you."

"And could every member of your fighting force?" Josh asked. "You need more people."

Briony nodded. "You're right, Josh, which is why I was wondering if there was a way to bring across more than just one werewolf. We all know how deadly they are to vampires here. There must be a way to reverse the rule that my father imposed on the gates. Can you look into it?"

"I already have," Sophie said. She looked slightly guilty about that, "for your sake."

Briony understood what she meant by that, and a wave of gratitude swept through her. Sophie had been looking for a way to let Kevin and Jake into Palisor? It was easy to forget now that the other woman was still her great aunt, and how much she loved her. Though as she was now, she would be an important weapon against the vampires too. Even back in Wicked, she had been the most dangerous vampire hunter there.

Briony almost didn't dare to ask. "Did you find a way?"

Sophie looked uncomfortable. "I'm sorry, Briony, but there is only one way, and we kind of already know it. A werewolf has to ascend to the throne of Palisor."

So it was the same as before. She'd have to marry Josh.

"So how does that help me?" she asked.

Sophie shook her head. "I'm sorry. All I know is that, until the strongest werewolf in the kingdom sits on the throne by force or marriage, you won't be able to open the gates."

And Josh was the only werewolf in Palisor, making him automatically the strongest. Which meant that there was only one way to control the gates and get help.

Josh wasn't the kind of person who gloated. Instead, he just nodded. "We don't have much time, but you're right. We need the strength of my werewolves if we're to have a chance of defeating these vampires. We're their natural enemy. You know that. You know the powers we have against them. So, Briony, what are you going to choose? Will you marry me?"

Briony looked around. She could see the way Fallon tensed, his expression blank in the way that meant he was trying to stop her seeing what he felt. Even Vigor seemed to be angry, his hands clenching into fists.

Josh obviously saw that reaction. "Don't you agree," he demanded, "that this is a time when we need unity? When our personal desires count for very little? Unlike you, I have never sought to have Briony for my own. This is simply a matter of what is best for everyone. Or don't you want to be able to fight off this threat?"

"Perhaps we can fight them ourselves," Vigor suggested.

"Really? You didn't do such a good job against Marcus' vampires." Josh looked back to Briony. "You have to choose, Briony. Do you want the werewolves here that you'll need, or not?"

"You know I don't have a choice," Briony said.

"Even though it will trigger the Vampire Apocalypse?" Fallon asked from the side. He was obviously struggling to control himself, but at the same time, he'd managed to make an important point.

Josh shrugged. "If it means saving the world…"

It seemed like an impossible position. If she didn't marry Josh, then Vigor's army would be overwhelmed, no matter how confident he was about their abilities. If she did, then she might be condemning Fallon, her brother, and every other good vampire to death.

"Is there no way around it?" Briony asked, turning to Sophie. If anyone knew, she would.

Her great aunt shook her head. Vigor seemed more optimistic though. "The marriage is only one of the conditions of the destruction of the vampires. There are others."

"So if I marry Josh it won't automatically mean them dying?" Briony asked. Even so, marrying *Josh*…

"I'm not a fate worse than death, Briony," Josh said, stepping close to her and taking her hand. This close, she could feel the sheer presence of him next to her, smell the masculine scent of him, and that scent fired something within her. She could feel attraction sweeping through her, and need. She shouldn't feel it, she knew that. She loved Kevin, not him, so Josh shouldn't be making her respond in exactly the same way. Yet even as she felt it, Briony knew what it was. Josh was an alpha wolf, and that meant that there would always be some part of her that would respond to him.

Archer interrupted. "Guys, do you want to hurry up, maybe? These monsters are fast. I don't need the telescope to see them now, which means we're going to need to get our troops together in a hurry if we don't want to end up being killed."

Briony looked in the direction where she'd seen the dark cloud through the telescope. She could make it out too now, swirling on the edge of what was visible from up in the palace. For a moment, the sheer speed of that frightened her, but she pushed that feeling aside. Her father had been able to force these creatures into the chasm. She had the same power. He had been the champion of Palisor, protecting it with his magic, but so was she now. She wasn't going to fail.

Chapter 12

They went down into the palace, rushing off about the tasks they needed to perform before the creatures from Xylyx got there. The dragons had to fly out messages, Vigor had to start to get his army together... pretty soon, it seemed that everyone except Briony had some kind of job to do. She, meanwhile found herself left alone in the room she'd woken up in earlier, where another dress was laid out by a silk screen patterned with images of battle.

Briony went behind it to get changed, and she was halfway into her new dress when she heard footsteps on the other side of it.

"Briony?"

It was Josh. Briony wasn't sure that there was much left to say to him. He'd manipulated her, using what he knew about Palisor to push her into a position that would give him more power.

"What do you want, Josh?" And more to the point, what did he want while she was still trying to lace up a dress that fastened at the back, meaning that no one without a servant to hand would ever be able to get into it? Who had these dresses been designed for? Princesses, probably.

"Actually, I wanted to apologize," Josh said. "I know that I've put you in a difficult position, and that you still aren't certain about marrying me. I know I'm not what you want."

"You could say that," Briony said. He wasn't *who* she wanted, at least.

"That's how fate works sometimes though," Josh said. "You'll have to make a decision soon, Briony. There isn't any time to waste."

So he wasn't just there to apologize. Or maybe he was, but even while he did something like that, Josh couldn't stop himself from trying to manipulate things. That thought made something flick over in Briony, and she made a decision. The decision she suspected she'd always known she'd make.

"I'm not marrying you, Josh."

"What?" Josh sounded genuinely surprised by that, like he really couldn't believe that she would do anything other than marry him. "But you have to-"

"No, I don't," Briony said, cutting him off. "The monsters from Xylyx don't change anything. The gates don't change anything. My father pushed the monsters back into the chasm before, without your werewolves. If he did it, then I can do it."

"I think you'll regret that," Josh said.

Briony sighed. "Get out, Josh."

She heard Josh go, but she wasn't thinking of him by then. He wasn't important enough to think about. Instead, she turned her attention back to the dress, though it still wouldn't lace right at the top. Maybe if she took the head of the scepter off for a moment? Briony unhooked it from around her neck, picking up the golden horn as well and putting them both down on the bed together. They touched, just barely, as she did it.

A shimmer of power ran along her skin, and Briony looked down just in time to see the horn and the scepter starting to glow. They glowed with golden light, the chain of the scepter stretched out by it so that it and the horn formed two sides of a triangle, with Briony on the third side. Light leapt around that triangle, bouncing from it in a complex web, then arcing into her in what felt like a shock of electricity.

Briony had felt this kind of power before, when she'd acquired the magic that had let her destroy Marcus, and when she'd transformed into the hugtandalfer that she was now. So what was this? Was it her coming into her full power as a hugtandalfer? As the queen of this land? Briony didn't know, and she didn't have the time to think about it, because in that moment the power of it overwhelmed her.

It poured through her, flashing along every nerve, making her muscles spasm as it flowed along her synapses. Briony let out a gasp as the power moved through her, hot and cold, pleasant and painful all at once. The unicorn had told her that with the horn, she would be the ultimate slayer. Briony had assumed that it was because the horn would be some kind of weapon for her, but what if it was more than that? What if it was actually *transforming* her? It certainly *felt* like it was transforming her like then, because Briony imagined that she could feel the cells of her body dissolving, changing, shifting as the power from the horn and the scepter touched them.

Suddenly, Briony found herself looking out from a spot that seemed to be far above Palisor, staring down at the land below where the darkness of the creatures from the chasm flowed. Briony could see them now, or some of them at least, because it was like they wrapped darkness around themselves, doing automatically the kind of thing that Pietre did with shadows. Only here, the goal didn't seem to be stealth. They simply hated the light so much that they carried literal darkness with them.

Some of them were humanoid, but barely so. They were monsters and things of nightmares, twisted so much beyond human or hugtandalfer shape that Briony could barely look at them. There were other creatures there too. Things with too many legs and insectoid carapaces. Things that slithered with lizard-like movements. It seemed like Xylyx held many dangers.

She turned away from that darkness, and found herself seeing something that shone. She wished that she could see it closer, and suddenly, she *was* closer. Close enough to see Vigor there, dressed in shining plate armor, a sword that shone silver in the sunlight in his hand. Around him were more hugtandalfer, arranged in ranks, armed with spears, swords and shields that gleamed so that they had to be visible from miles away. They were here on the road below the palace, not clinging to the rocks to defend, but going out to meet the threat. Briony felt a surge of pride at that bravery, but also worry. Wouldn't it be safe for Vigor and his troops to fight with high walls and higher mountain slopes to protect them.

Then she was high up again, over the land, and Briony saw why they couldn't. She saw the villages and the small farms in the path of the onrushing darkness. Yes, they could sit in the palace and wait for the creatures from Xylyx to come to them, but what would the vampires and the worse creatures do then? Who could predict what they would do, when they were rumored to be no more than animals? They might lay waste to the land without ever coming near the palace to fight. Vigor had done the only thing he could in going out to meet them.

Briony blinked, and she was back in her room again. The horn and the scepter were no longer glowing, and she found herself wondering if what she'd just seen was real, or if it was just imagination produced by having that much power coursing through her.

"Here, let me help with that."

Briony hadn't heard Sophie come in, but now she moved over to Briony, pulling tight the last few stays on the dress.

"There," she said. "You look beautiful."

Sophie looked more military than beautiful. She'd tied her hair back severely, and she'd acquired silver steel armor that was a mixture of open chainmail and solid plate. She wore a pair of swords strapped to her hip, short enough and slender enough that they were more like long knives.

"Where are you going?" Briony asked. "You're going out to fight?"

Sophie nodded. "I need to go join Vigor's army. He's already outside with them, moving to cut off the creatures."

So Briony *had* seen them. She wondered what that meant, and exactly what the horn and the scepter had done to her. For now though she didn't say anything about what had just happened. She wasn't the one who was about to go out to face an army of creatures even more evil than Marcus' vampires had been.

"You're looking worried," Sophie said.

"I'm just worried about you, if you're going to go out there."

"I have to," Sophie replied. "Vigor's army... they're brave, and they're strong. They're hugtandalfer too, and that means they're going to be strong and fast. But they don't have my experience of fighting vampires. They need me to go out and help. *Vigor* needs me."

"You really like him, don't you?" Briony said.

Sophie smiled. "He's sweet."

"Sweet?" If there was one adjective Briony would never have applied to her too formal and dour step-brother, that was it. Briony sighed. "Just promise me that you'll be careful."

"Oh, I'm always careful," Sophie said. She moved forward to hug Briony, enveloping her in her arms and pressing her tight to the silver steel of her armor. "And whatever you decide when it comes to Josh and your destiny, know that I love you and I want you to be happy in all things."

"Josh?" Briony had put him completely out of her mind. "Are you saying that you think I should marry him?"

Sophie smiled. "It means whatever you want it to mean. Do I have to spell these things out? You need to trust your own judgment more, darling."

"What if I get it wrong?" Briony asked. "People could die."

"Trust yourself," Sophie insisted. "You have all the power of your father and in the scepter you have the power of your ancestors. You've been trained by, I'd like to think, the best slayer around. You've proven yourself against Pietre. You reduced Marcus to ashes. You have a weapon in that horn that Vigor tells me is incredibly powerful, and you have all the magic that goes with that. You have all the resources you need to succeed, but you're the one who has to choose what you're going to do."

Briony stepped back from her great-aunt, nodding. "Then there isn't going to be a wedding. Not today. Not that there would be the time for it. We have a battle to fight instead. You're right, I do need to make these decisions. Help me get out of this dress, Sophie, and find me some armor."

"Why?" Sophie asked, sounding suspicious. "You aren't planning to-"

"I can sit in here waiting for you, Vigor and the others to solve my problems, or I can go out and deal with them myself," Briony said. "I'm not going to sit in here waiting for the creatures of Xylyx to come over the walls. If you lose, then they'll come here and they'll kill everyone who waits behind. It's better to be out there fighting. At least there I can help."

"But-"

"You were just telling me how much power I had," Briony pointed out. She shifted the golden horn in her hand, working out what kind of weapon it would be. "Well, I want to use it. I'm going to use it. Now, could you please help me find some armor? I don't want to go into the middle of a battle in just a dress."

Sophie stood there, hesitating for several seconds, obviously trying to think of a way to keep Briony safe. Finally though, she gave in and nodded.

"I'll go down to the armory to see what's left."

Chapter 13

Sophie went off to fetch armor for Briony, and while she did that, Archer and Fletcher came into her room together. Fletcher nodded to her, while Archer moved forward, reaching out to put a hand on her shoulder. His touch was light and surprisingly warm as Briony looked him in the eye. The dragon looked a little uncomfortable.

"I wanted to say, my queen, that it has been a pleasure being your dragon."

There was something about the way he said that. It worried Briony. "You're talking like you aren't expecting to be around me much longer."

"I will stay beside you, whatever happens," Archer said, "but this threat is a dangerous one." He paused, looking back at Fletcher. "I will stay, but Fletcher is going. One of us has to alert the rest of the dragons of Palisor."

"I thought there were plenty of dragons around here?" Briony said.

Archer shrugged. "Some, but most of us do not serve hugtandalfer or live among them. There are whole clans of our kind in the mountains." Archer smiled. "I have a big family, and they all have power. They're all loyal to Palisor too. Fletcher should be able to bring a few of them back with him."

"How many?" Briony asked.

"Enough, maybe," Archer replied. "I heard that you're not marrying Josh. That means no werewolves, so we're going to need all the dragons we can get. Maybe there will be enough to turn the tide. I hope so."

Briony nodded. She knew how difficult the absence of the werewolves would make things, yet she couldn't make her decisions based on just that. The only question now was whether they would be able to fill the gap left by the werewolves' absence.

"Are you sure?" she asked. "I mean, I'm sure you have plenty of family, but with the scale of what's out there..."

Fletcher stepped forward. "I will be able to fetch you dragons, your majesty. My blood goes back to that of the oldest dragons, when they ruled this land."

Briony vaguely remembered that story, that the hugtandalfer had used magic to control the dragons and bond with them, taking control of Palisor from them.

"You're saying the two of you are some kind of dragon royalty?" Briony asked.

Archer shook his head. "No. There is no dragon royalty anymore."

"But if there were," Fletcher said, "then Archer and I would be it."

Archer glanced across to him, and it was obvious this was an argument the two dragons had had before.

"What?" Fletcher demanded. He returned his attention to Briony. "I'll get you your dragons."

With that, he left, obviously in a hurry to fetch his relatives and the rest of the dragons.

"Well," Briony said, "that's one piece of good news, at least."

Archer nodded. "So, we have a full on battle coming up, and we'll have dragons. Now what? Where do we go from here?"

Briony was going to point out that she wasn't sure either, but she guessed that, as the ruler there, she didn't get to admit that. In any case, Sophie arrived back then with the armor and weapons for her to prepare for the battle. She took Briony behind the screen in her room again, helping her to change.

There was chainmail. There was padding that went under the chainmail. There were greaves, bracers and other sections of light but solid plate. There was a long jacket that looked suspiciously like the one Sophie had left Wicked in, that came complete with pockets and hangers for stakes and knives.

Briony was already rushing to get into armor and to get what she needed to fight. She had the unicorn's horn as a weapon, but she wasn't sure how much the legend holds true in a time of battle. She placed a jacket on herself that she recognized from Sophie's stash of slayer weapons. The jacket had stake holders sewn into it so she can carry a few wooden stakes in it.

More than a few, in fact. There was a belt loop for the golden horn too, and Briony wore it like a sword, slung from her waist.

"Use it, but don't rely on it," Sophie said. "It's an untested weapon. It ought to be a deadly one if the myths are true, but until we know for sure, don't risk your life by trying to use it as your only weapon. Use the stakes, or use your magic. The kind of fireball that finished Marcus should work."

Briony nodded. "I will," she promised, though even as she promised it, she could feel a strange kind of confidence in the back of her mind that the golden horn would work. She just needed to have the courage to use it.

"I thought you had more sense than to throw yourself into something like this."

Briony stepped out from behind the screen to see Josh standing there.

"Isn't all this a bit extreme to keep from marrying me?" he asked. "Getting suited up in armor and putting your life at risk?"

"I would have done that anyway," Briony insisted.

Josh looked at her for several seconds. "Yes, I believe you would." He sighed. "If I could get my werewolves here, I would, regardless of the marriage thing. I know we need to win here to keep Wicked safe, and my people with it. I want that. All right, so I wanted the power, and I wanted you too. What man wouldn't? But I want them safe."

Briony didn't know what to say to that. Particularly to the compliment. She'd assumed that Josh was only interested in her for what she had to offer in terms of power. Josh went on then though.

"That's why I'm going to do what we both know you want me to do, Briony."

"I don't want you to do anything, Josh."

Josh shook his head. "You do. You just haven't been able to ask for it, because you keep your word. You want Kevin, and we both need my werewolves to be able to come through. Archer here can find me a gate. I'll go back through, and Kevin can come here. If you decide to marry him, then he'll be a worthy enough werewolf for the scepter. It should mean that you're able to control the gates again and let more of my kind through."

"Oh Josh," Briony said. "I don't know what to say. I guess I owe you an apology for thinking you were…"

Josh raised his hand, and Briony was immediately reminded that Josh was a king, the Werewolf King.

"Utterly power mad? I can see why you'd think it, but for me, power is always about a purpose, and that purpose is keeping my people safe. And of course, since I know you will never marry me, but you might marry Kevin, this way is our best shot at getting back into Palisor."

Briony smiled. "Nice to know that the old you is in there somewhere, working out the angles."

"It's what a ruler has to do, Briony," Josh said. "Now, I'll need Archer's help."

Briony nodded to Archer, who went with Josh out the window, transforming and taking the werewolf king with him.

"We should be going too," Sophie said.

Briony nodded. "I'll be there in a minute.

Sophie nodded and headed out the door. Fallon came in through it as she left. He crossed the distance to Briony in two quick strides, pulling her into his arms and kissing her deeply.

"That's for deciding not to marry Josh," he said, before kissing her again. "And that's for all those good vampires who have just narrowly avoided the vampire apocalypse thanks to you."

He seemed so happy then, and Briony could guess why. He thought that he still had a chance with her. Who knew, maybe he did, but right then, it didn't seem very likely. She hadn't told him yet about the plan as it currently stood, where she would marry Kevin and that would be that. Did he deserve to know? Even though Archer had told her that the marriage was only one of the keys to the vampire apocalypse, did Fallon have a right to know that Briony was thinking of taking one step closer to it to save her kingdom?

No, not yet. She couldn't tell Fallon yet, and not just because it would hurt him too much at a time when he seemed so happy for once. The truth was that nothing was settled right then. Josh had gone off to get Kevin, but who was to say whether the werewolf king would be able to get him to come? Maybe they wouldn't find a gate. Maybe Kevin wouldn't believe him.

Or maybe he wouldn't want to come. Briony had seen him in the reflecting pool with Carol. If she asked him to marry her, and that was still an if, even with her, then would he say yes? It was obvious that he was interested in Carol, and she was a werewolf like him. Maybe Kevin hadn't wanted to wait around in Wicked for her. Maybe he'd decided that he was tired of waiting for Briony to make up her mind between him and Fallon. Briony knew how jealous she'd felt when she'd seen Carol and him.

But there was one note of hope even as she thought that. Despite the jealousy and the flash of anger that had run through her seeing Kevin there with Carol, Briony still wanted him. She still loved him. If she felt that way, then couldn't he? Maybe? She shook her head. This wasn't the time to think about that. There was a battle that needed fighting. For now though, she knew she had to keep all this from Fallon. She wasn't going to hurt him over something that might not even happen.

"Are you going to join in the battle?" Briony asked.

Fallon nodded. "And it looks like you're planning to be in the middle of the fighting."

"Maybe not the middle," Briony said, "but the unicorn died for a purpose, and I'm not going to stand around with its horn, not using it for anything when I could be helping."

Fallon nodded then, though Briony could see the worry in his expression too. "This is going to be dangerous,

Briony. At least as dangerous as anything else we've ever faced."

"I know," Briony said, "but this time, we'll have a whole army to back us up."

"It makes a change from trying to do everything with a few werewolves and the members of the Preservation Society," Fallon said. He turned serious again for a moment. "I'll be watching out for you in the fight, Briony. Wherever you go, I go. I'm not letting you out of my sight. I couldn't stand it if…"

Briony wanted to promise him that nothing bad would happen to her, but she didn't. She'd learned that much at least over the past few months. Bad things happened to people. All you could do was try to deal with it and make sure that they didn't happen to anyone else.

"I'll be looking out for you too, Fallon," Briony promised. She hefted the horn. "Come on. Sophie will be waiting for us outside."

Chapter 14

Josh clung to Archer while the dragon searched for a gate, hating being so high off the ground with so little between him and almost certain death if he fell. He felt out of control like this, and he hated being out of control. He hated being someone who had events dictated to him rather than making his own choices. Yet Briony did this all the time.

Archer was circling now, and Josh guessed that he'd found something. A glance down confirmed that. The pale arch of a gate stood in the middle of a patch of open ground, not glowing with shining mist yet, but Josh knew that it would with a dragon around. And then they'd be able to go through. Hopefully. There was only one real problem.

The creatures of Xylyx swarmed around the base of the gate, the darkness they carried with them swirling around them like waist high tendrils of mist. As Archer flew lower above them, Josh could make out more and more of them. They were grotesque. There were none of the strangest creatures from the chasm there, but the vampires there were enough. And they were vampires, that much was obvious as they looked up at the two of them circling above, their fangs clear to see.

Yet they were different from any vampires Josh had seen before, too. They were, hunched and muscular, in clothing of a black material that Josh didn't know seeming so close to human and yet so far away from it. Pietre's vampires looked normal to the untrained eye, and even Marcus' had looked like something out of human history, but these? They looked like something sub-human. Pre-human. Something that had never been human. Their eyes were the red of a vampire in the greatest depths of hunger and their fingernails were claws as long and sharp as those of a big cat. They would never have passed for human. And they were in the way of the gate. Josh shivered involuntarily.

He shivered more as Archer brought them down at the edge of the horde, transforming into his human form there.

"What are you doing?" Josh demanded as a few of the creatures on the edges of the mob of vampires started to turn their attention towards them. "Can't you just fly over them?"

"I have to bring the gate to power," Archer said. "Get ready to run."

"I thought it was only Briony who could do that? Hugtandalfer royalty at least."

"Get ready to *run!*" Archer repeated.

Josh swallowed his fear. He wasn't going to give into this. He was the king of the werewolves. Vampires, even a horde of impossibly primitive ones, were *not* going to intimidate him. Although it helped that they were still at least a hundred yards away. Far enough that although he could see the glow of their eyes and the yellow of their curving fangs, they couldn't hurt him yet.

"Of all the places to have a gate," Josh muttered before transforming. If he was going to have to run through this horde, he certainly wasn't going to do it in human form. He was faster as a wolf. Stronger as a wolf. There wasn't anyone *as* fast or strong. Except possibly Kevin, and even that thought didn't give Josh the surge of anger that it usually did. He'd done what he needed to do. He'd come here and he'd found a way that would let the rest of his people come too. Briony would never accept him, so going home was better. At home, he could take his throne back. At home he could look after his people.

The world looked so different as a wolf. Color was less important like this. *Vision* was less important. Instead, sight, smell and more primal senses blended so that the whole world reached him in a rush. How many people were lucky enough to see the world like this? How many had seen it like this almost from birth, the way he had.

"I'm opening the gate," Archer said, and spread his hands. Josh looked out over the horde of creatures from Xylyx, and he could see the mist starting to rise in the gateway. He howled.

"We don't want them getting through," Archer said. "We have to hurry."

Josh hadn't thought of that, and he cursed himself for not doing so. Normally, he had things worked out to the last detail, but here, he'd forgotten. When they went through, it would leave a gap. A gap into which vampires could step even if they didn't possess the scepter the way

Marcus had. Which meant that they might be dragging a whole battalion of vampires back with them. Even if that was true though, could they afford not to do it? To look for another chance?

"Run now!" Archer ordered, and that made up Josh's mind for him. He sprinted, and Archer sprinted forward in front of him, somehow reaching the vampires first. He didn't stop to try to fight them, but just kept moving, sliding into gaps between them, moving like smoke as they tried to grab him. In seconds, Archer was at the gate, and then through it.

Josh sprinted to try to keep up. If the vampires were so crazed that they didn't care about a dragon running through them, then he ought to find this easy. He ran as fast as he could, keeping his head low and plunging towards the gate ahead of him. Unfortunately, that meant plunging into the darkness that still swirled around the vampires. It only came up to their waists now, but that meant that it was higher than Josh's head. He ran through it anyway.

The darkness was absolute. He couldn't see, and with his other senses overwhelmed by the clamor and the stink of the vampires all around him, Josh was effectively blind in every way. All he could do was plow forward, relying on the fact that the gate was somewhere there ahead of him.

He thought he could hear whispers in the darkness. Not voices exactly, or at least not voices speaking any language he knew, but something. A strain of hatred and violence; malevolence directed not at him, but at everything. There was something in the darkness that wove between the vampires. Something that wove them together into a kind of bestial tapestry. Something that took these violent, maddened beasts and made something more of them.

Right then though, Josh didn't care about any of that. He didn't care about anything except keeping moving, running with all the power that his werewolf form had at its disposal, heading for the gate before any of the vampires could understand that they had a werewolf in their midst.

Something grabbed at his hind legs, and he knew that it was too late.

Josh spun, knowing that it had to be one of the vampires. As he spun, the darkness seemed to clear a little, for no good reason Josh could see, except maybe that it let the vampire attacking him terrify its prey with the sight of it. At close range, that was terrifying. A hairless, powerful, ugly thing with fangs like daggers, its clawed hands fastened on Josh's legs. But Josh wasn't anyone's prey.

He lashed out, biting the hands that held him, clamping down with his jaws and rending briefly to force the vampire to let go. He was pleased to see the creature bleeding, dark, almost red-black blood dripping from the wounds. Yet the vampire didn't let go. Didn't this creature feel pain? Josh knew that vampires could be tough, but mostly, they knew about it when a werewolf bit them. Josh bit down again, this time feeling the crunch of bone beneath his teeth as his jaws bore down with enough force that they almost tore away one of the hands holding him. Still, somehow, the vampire clung on. It was incredible. Almost like it didn't have enough of a mind to care about what happened to it. Was there nothing that could stop these ones?

Almost as if the thought made it happen, the vampire reared back, screaming like a wounded animal. Whatever it was in a werewolf's saliva that made it deadly to vampires in Palisor obviously still worked on these new ones, because Josh could see the tracery of black lines running up along its veins as the venom did its work. The creature screamed, and then burst into brief, magnesium bright flames.

A surge of hope flashed through Josh, as fast as the fire before it. He hadn't had the chance to use this power in Palisor, but feeling it now, he could see all that it could do. He'd spent so long trying to find a way to keep his people safe, and this... this was something that might be able to do it. With this bite, a werewolf didn't have to succeed in attacking the throat or driving home a stake. With this, they were *better* than vampires.

The darkness had closed in again by then though, and Josh realized with a start that he didn't know which way the gate was anymore. Panic threatened to replace the hope, until with a harsh bark that would have been a laugh had he been human, Josh realized there was one easy way to solve that problem. He darted forward, and the moment he made contact with something in the dark, he bit down. A few frantic seconds later, the screaming started, and after that...

The darkness parted in the bright blue flare of the dying vampire. By that light, Josh saw the way he had to run, and he didn't hesitate. He had to get there before vampires could get through. Before the gate could close. They were so unpredictable, after all. His muscles bunched, and he ran. He ran as fast as he had ever run, while around him, Josh felt a shift in the Xylyx vampires. They were coming for him. That or they were trying to get through the gate, and Josh didn't know which thought was more terrifying. He pushed himself harder still.

He leapt, and he saw an arm reaching out from the gate. Archer's arm. Josh transformed in midair, flinging out his hand, wrapping his fingers around the dragon's. Archer dragged him through, pulling him onto soft grass beyond, in a very familiar looking meadow with a stream in it.

Archer jerked his hand, and the gate disappeared.

Josh lay there panting, staring up at Archer and trying to think. Had the dragon really just made a gate disappear? He hadn't thought that was possible. He was sure that, if it were, Archer would have done it before now. Yet he'd just seen him do it. Had he gained something through his connection to Briony? Had he given her something?

Josh thought he could see the shape of it then. Archer was another piece of the puzzle. A puzzle with who knew how many pieces. He was the key to opening and closing the gates, a dragon bound to the blood heir to Palisor. Archer was special enough without all that; he was a *dragon* after all, but now it seemed to Josh like he might be the key to more than just the gate. He might be one of the keys to unlocking the whole complicated mess around Briony.

And he was currently in Wicked, on the other side of the gate from her.

Chapter 15

Kevin made his way through the forest in wolf form, hunting now. Carol had insisted on it, saying that they needed to prove their strength by taking on Pietre's vampires where they could find them, and honestly, Kevin didn't mind that so much. Any new vampires Pietre had made had to be hunted down before they could start killing people. That was simply the way things had to be. What he didn't like was the way Carol had backed him into a corner. If he wanted to draw Josh back, he had to play the part of the werewolves' king, and that meant doing what she said.

In this case, it meant stalking a small group of vampires with her. Just her, because Carol had decided that it would look weak for them to take too many other wolves. Or maybe she'd just wanted an excuse to get Kevin alone. Either way, she was stalking along beside him, closing in on a quartet of vampires who were all obviously young and confused about what had happened to them. Kids, transformed by Pietre or his creatures. Not that it changed anything.

He and Carol rushed forward, splitting as they attacked to make it look like they were going for separate targets, then charging towards a young male vampire in dark clothing. Carol hit him at knee height, while Kevin went higher, attacking his throat. Because the vampire was falling, he didn't have the chance to block Kevin's lunge at him, and maybe he hadn't learnt to defend that single vulnerability yet anyway. Kevin's jaws clamped around his throat and crushed down. The vampire died instantly.

The two of them split their attack then. Kevin went after the largest of the group, a boy who had clearly been a jock before being transformed. He even wore a letter jacket, and judging by the size of him, he'd probably played plenty of football. Kevin slammed into him anyway, expecting that the young vampire wouldn't be able to deal with the ferocity of his attack.

Maybe the kid was quicker than he looked though, because he managed to twist out of the way of that first attack enough to keep Kevin from getting his jaws around his throat. Kevin drove into him, knocking him backwards, and the vampire rolled before trying to take off into the woods. Kevin twisted suddenly, knowing that he should focus on the remaining ones.

There were two, one male, one female. Carol was attacking the female one, who was hissing in an animal mixture of rage and fear while lashing out with nails that had grown to claw length. Her fangs were out too, and Carol was having to hang back, being careful while she looked for an opening. Unless she could get the throat cleanly, even most new vampires would heal too quickly for wounds elsewhere to stop them.

The last of the male vampires was circling around, trying to get behind Carol. Kevin leapt at him, catching him from the side. Like the jock, it wasn't quite a clean hit, and the vampire managed to roll. Unlike the jock, this one kept fighting, its nails and fangs extending just as the girl's had. The vampire stepped back, swiping the air with those fingers as though testing them out for the first time. Kevin pressed forward, forcing him back into the trees. He didn't like leaving Carol like that, but she could handle a single vampire alone.

Kevin snapped at and harried the vampire he was fighting, not standing in one spot for more than a second, using the trees to his advantage as he dodged between them, attacking in sudden rushes. It was simply a question of judging his moment… there! Kevin leapt forward, his jaws closing on the throat of the vampire he was chasing, ending its existence with a single powerful bite.

He turned back towards the spot where Carol had been fighting, expecting her to have finished off the vampire she was battling against by then. She had, but what Kevin saw made him start forward. Carol was on the ground, while the jock vampire Kevin had driven off was standing over her, ready to bring his claws down in a vicious strike. He'd obviously doubled back, probably attacking Carol from behind, because that was the only way Kevin could think of that he'd be able to defeat her.

Kevin knew he had to do something, but even with his werewolf speed, he knew he wouldn't be able to cover the ground in time. Carol was obviously too hurt or stunned to move out of the way, too. That thought made Kevin want to cry out, or do *something*. It wasn't that he loved Carol, but he still didn't want her dead. Especially not when she was just about the only way for him to force Josh back here and get to Briony. Yet what could he do now? Kevin's mind raced, trying to think of an answer.

A dark furred form shot out of the trees, slamming into the back of the vampire. Its jaws clamped around the creature's neck and even from where he was standing, Kevin heard the snap of breaking bone. Right then though, he wasn't looking at the vampire. He was too busy looking at the new wolf. He *knew* that wolf.

Kevin transformed, stepping forward into the space between the trees. Carol had transformed too, and was standing there, scowling down at the newcomer.

"Now? *Now* you come back?"

Josh transformed, and stood there smiling faintly at his sister while the vampire on the ground burned to nothing. "It looks like it was just as well I did. I must say that your new boyfriend hasn't done a good job of keeping you in one piece."

"Not my boyfriend," Carol said pointedly. "My fiancé."

Josh looked from her to Kevin and back again. His eyes narrowed slightly. "Ah, I see." He started to take a step towards Kevin, and then seemed to think again, looking back towards Carol in obvious surprise. "I never thought you'd do something like that, Carol."

"You weren't here," she snapped at him.

"And now I am. We'll talk later about this."

Kevin started to step forward to intervene, but he stopped as another figure entered the small space between the trees. Archer looked around, seeming almost disappointed that the fight was over.

"Josh, we have to hurry."

Josh glanced at him. "Yes, you're right. Kevin, I'm here to fetch you. You have to go with Archer."

And Archer rarely left Briony's side now. "Briony's here?" Kevin asked.

"Briony is back in Palisor," Josh explained, "and she needs you. Well, she needs a werewolf, and unfortunately, I'm not the one she wants." He looked genuinely disappointed by that, but recovered well. "And of course, you going to Briony solves a great many problems."

"Like the threat of me marrying Carol?" Kevin asked.

Josh flashed him an angry look. "Yes. But I can live with that now. There are more important things. Go, Kevin. Go, or I'll assume that you actually mean to fight for my sister."

"I don't need anyone to fight for me," Carol said.

"I'm starting to see that," Josh said, "though I think you'd be in trouble if I hadn't before."

Carol snorted. "I'd have dealt with it."

That actually got a small smile from Josh. "Of course you would."

Kevin didn't have the time for that. "Josh, what's going on? What made you leave Palisor? Why are you back?"

Josh looked at him and shrugged. "There are dangerous things going on. A... I guess you could call it a kind of prison, for some of the most evil creatures on Palisor has opened up. I don't have all the details, but I do know that without more help, Palisor will fall. And then so will Wicked. Briony won't do what is needed with me. Perhaps she will with you."

"And what's needed?" Kevin asked.

Josh shook his head. "Ask her that when you get there. Just make sure you don't fail. All of us are counting on you."

Kevin looked at Josh for several seconds. Could this be some kind of plan on the werewolf leader's part? No, Kevin couldn't see how it could be, except inasmuch as it got him his throne back, and Josh had been quick enough to step away from that. As far as he could tell, this was genuinely about trying to help Palisor and Wicked.

Kevin nodded. "Alright. I'll go. And… thank you, Josh."

The words were hard to get out, but he managed them. Across from him, Carol looked furious.

"Just like that, you're going to Palisor?" she demanded. "You're going to abandon me? It's always her, isn't it?"

"It's always Briony for me," Kevin agreed.

"You-"

But by then, Kevin was already running. He could guess at how much that would hurt Carol, but he had more important things to think about. She'd tried to use him for her own ends, and as far as he was concerned she and her brother were welcome to one another. He was just interested in getting back to Briony.

"Which way?" he yelled as Archer caught up with him.

The dragon pointed. "Down there. I closed the gate after us when we came through, but there's a spot that will open again. I can feel it."

Kevin didn't argue with that. He knew that the dragons could find gates, though how they were going to open it when they got there, he didn't know. Were they going to be stuck here, locked out of Palisor? They came into a clearing that had all the markers of a gate, from the small stream and the wild flowers to the brightly colored trees and the general feeling of peace.

Archer gestured with his hand and to Kevin's shock, mist sprang up, forming itself into the familiar shape of an arching gate to Palisor. When had he acquired the ability to do that? Did it even matter, just so long as Archer was providing him with a way to get back to Briony? He stood there, watching as the mist within the gate shimmered and cleared, revealing the landscape beyond it. The gate hadn't done *that* for anyone but Briony before, either.

Kevin stood there staring at what lay beyond the gate. It was hard not to, because what lay beyond was a battle. Dragons wheeled across the sky, strafing the ground with white hot gouts of flame that reflected off the brightly metallic colors of their scales. Below, creatures surged and milled, enveloped in a mist like darkness that seemed to shift and follow them as they scattered before the flames. They looked like vampires, but not any vampires Kevin had seen before. These ones were hairless and angular, muscled but moving differently than anything human.

Other things moved with them, utterly impossible things that crawled and slithered and in some cases flew, flitting up towards the dragons in an attempt to bring them down. One dragon did fall, plummeting to earth like a fallen meteorite, crashing into the ground while the creatures around it swarmed over it. In a matter of seconds, they left nothing but bones.

"The vampires of Xylyx," Archer said, and the dragon shuddered.

"We have to go through into that?" Kevin asked.

Archer nodded. "It's the way back to Briony."

When Archer put it like that, it wasn't even a choice. Kevin took a breath and threw himself forward through the gate, ready to fight his way through whatever lay beyond.

Chapter 16

The battle around them was chaos. Tendrils of darkness flowed between vampires as they skittered and scrambled forward, attacking dragon and hugtandalfer alike. Kevin shifted form as one came for him, barely dodging the sweep of clawed hands and clamping his teeth down on the creature's leg. It was such a different way of fighting here in Palisor than it was back in Wicked. It was so much simpler, when any bite could kill a vampire.

It needed to be. The next vampire was already rushing at him as the first one burst into bright flames. It was fast. Almost too fast for Kevin to avoid, passing within inches of him. He barely managed to catch it with his teeth as it shot past him, but that was enough. The creature stood there for several seconds before it started screaming and the flames finally claimed it.

Archer transformed alongside him, his natural form shining golden in the midst of the darkness around him. He swept his tail to one side, knocking back vampires, then followed it with a burst of flame that swept over half a dozen of them at once, consuming them in a matter of moments.

More swept in, and more after that. Kevin leapt clear of a blow, only to take a kick to the side from a second vampire. He spun and lashed out with his teeth, leaving the vampire to die, but by then he was already trying to defend against an attack from two more vampires. Kevin shifted back to his human form just long enough to throw one of them over his hip, kicked backwards to knock the second of them away and changed back into wolf form to try to finish the first with a bite. By then though, it had already spun away into the greater melee.

Kevin didn't know what to make of these vampires. They were strong, as strong as Marcus' vampires had been, and they were fast, but there was also something almost mindlessly savage about them. They didn't seem to think. They just charged into the attack. And in a lot of ways, that made them far more dangerous. At least with Marcus, they'd been able to reason with him. With these… they just kept coming, not seeming to care about their safety. Not seeming to care about anything except blood and violence.

Kevin managed to pull back from the fight for a second as Archer let loose a second gout of flame. He looked around, trying to work out where they were, and saw that they were in a hilly environment, with a tree lined path leading up the rocky slopes, and at the top of it there was what looked like a castle, so skillfully built onto the peak of the cliff it sat on that it seemed to be part of it.

Between them and the castle there was an army that shone silver on the ground and every color of the rainbow above it. The hugtandalfer warriors were there, along with their dragons, and they were definitely in the middle of a hard fight. As Kevin watched, the darkness around the vampires swept forward and they moved with it, seizing a hugtandalfer woman from the end of the line. She screamed, loud enough that Kevin could hear her above the rest of the battle, but not for long.

Briony would be there somewhere. Briony, Fallon and the rest of them. They just had to get to them. Kevin started forward, biting the first vampire to get in his way, dodging around the second, and starting back as the third was engulfed in a jet of flame thrown out by Archer. They fought their way forward like that, working in tandem. Archer blasted vampires with his fire and Kevin did his best to keep the dragon from being swarmed by vampires. One on one, he was more than a match for them, but Archer was also a large, slow target in his dragon form. Kevin had to run in circles around him, biting any vampire that came too close while using Archer as a shelter against the worst of their attacks. Slowly, gradually, they began to move forward.

Then Kevin saw her, not at the heart of the fighting, because the other hugtandalfer moved around her to stop that happening, but still staking vampires left and right, using a stake that seemed to shine strangely golden. Briony. She was there on the hill with the others, Fallon fighting right beside her. They just had to get to her now.

Yet that was easier said than done. There were hundreds of vampires between them. Vampires that would be even more dangerous when night finally fell, because then they would be able to come at the hugtandalfer from all angles, unseen. Kevin pushed forward, biting vampires left and right. Archer lashed out with his tail and used his flame to blast groups of vampires, as well as firing it at some of the stranger things that seemed to scuttle among them. Had they been things that the vampires had found down in their chasm prison? Whatever they were, they seemed as mindless and vicious as the vampires themselves.

The vampires seemed almost confused by the idea that he and Archer were there, in the middle of them. They were focused on the hugtandalfer in front of them, rushing forward in waves, seemingly uncaring whether they lived or died. There were so many of them. Enough that every time the hugtandalfer fought off one group, another was there to attack. Kevin saw hugtandalfer fighting, swinging swords and glaives left and right at the kind of speeds that no human would have been able to match. Yet the vampires matched them, so that the fights took on a frantic quality. A hugtandalfer might cut down one of the vampires as it emerged from the darkness they carried with them, but there was always another one ready to take its place.

Kevin saw them dying there. A hugtandalfer went down with three vampires atop him. A dragon that swooped in too low when trying to burn the vampires was pulled to earth and swarmed in a way that made Kevin even more careful about protecting Archer from attack. He spun, snapping at a vampire that had come too close to the golden dragon, while Archer spat a wall of flame that caught a cluster of vampires as they charged him.

Perhaps if there had been more werewolves there, the battle wouldn't have been a difficult one. The Wickham pack, given the same powers Kevin had, would have made short work even of the horde of vampires that surrounded them. Yet there was only Kevin, loping from vampire to vampire, biting and moving as flares of bright light from dying vampires marked his passage.

The chaos of the battle was absolute by then. The noise was overwhelming as hugtandalfers screamed, dragons roared, and the vampires made inhuman sounds of their own. Fire was all around as the dragons strafed the vampires' ranks. There was the clash of claws on steel armor, the thud of weapons hitting flesh. There was the scent of death and burning in the air, mingled with the rank, ever present stench of the vampires. Kevin kept going even though his limbs ached with the effort. How long had they been fighting now? An hour, more? How long would it be until sundown?

It was hard to tell how the battle was going. The only bodies on the ground were those of hugtandalfers and dragons. The fire that engulfed the vampires on their deaths made it impossible to tell how many of those they'd killed. All Kevin knew was that suddenly, as he looked up, he was closer to Briony than he'd thought. She'd obviously seen him too, because she started to fight her way forward.

Kevin ran for her, snapping at any vampire that got in his way. Behind him, he heard Archer take to the air, obviously deciding that Kevin could protect himself now. Kevin sprinted, arriving at Briony's side as she reached the last of the trees along the path and bringing down a vampire that leapt at her. Kevin transformed, and for a moment it seemed like there wasn't a battle raging in the background. Or maybe the hugtandalfer forces had simply succeeded in pushing the fight's front line out beyond them for a while.

Kevin didn't care. He didn't even care that Briony was wearing blood covered armor. He just drew her into his arms, kissing her deeply.

"I'm so glad you're okay," he said. "You sent Josh back. You sent him, just to fetch me."

"I love you," Briony said, pulling back just enough to look him in the eye. She hesitated, but not for long. "You know the ring you gave me as a sign that we were together?"

Kevin knew it. He had it on a chain around his neck. "Yes?"

"I want to wear it again."

Kevin hurried to remove it from the chain, slipping it onto one of her fingers.

"No," Briony said. "Not that finger."

"I don't understand," Kevin said. Or at least, he didn't dare to hope-

"Kevin," Briony said, "I love you. Even with the age difference between us. Even with you being a werewolf, and me being the queen of a completely different world. People have been telling me that I need to marry someone if I'm going to come into my full powers. Well, there's only one person I could ever want to marry."

"Don't ask to marry me just for that," Kevin said.

"I'm not," Briony assured him. "I'm asking to marry you because I want to spend the rest of my life with you. Okay, so I want to do it right now because it might be nice to actually *have* some rest of my life, but that doesn't make what I feel any less real."

Kevin didn't know what to say. Well there was one obvious thing. "Yes. Yes, I'll marry you. If you're sure?"

"I'm sure," Briony said.

"I always thought I'd be the one proposing," Kevin said, "and I don't think I'd have planned it like this..." he gestured to take in the battle going on behind them. Briony stepped past him, lancing the long, golden stake she held through a vampire.

"Me either," she said. "I'd thought I'd wait, at least until I was in college. Maybe longer. But this... this changes things, and honestly, no matter how long I wait, it will still be you, Kevin. It's *always* been you."

"And right now, we need to do this if we're going to save Palisor, don't we?" Kevin didn't mind that part so much now. He kissed Briony again, deeper this time.

"So that's a yes, then?" Briony asked with a smile, as they pulled apart.

"Yes," Kevin assured her, "it's a yes. Did you think I'd say anything else?"

"Maybe for a moment, when I saw you with Carol."

"And now?"

"Now, you're all mine," Briony said, kissing him.

Behind them, there was a pointed cough. Kevin turned to see Briony's Aunt Sophie bearing down on them.

"This is all very nice, and I'm very happy for you, but if you're serious about getting married, you might want to find some very quick vows. I hate to be the one to say this, but... we're losing this battle."

"We're not losing," Vigor said, appearing out of the throng to stand beside her. "It's a momentary setback."

"We're losing," Sophie said. "And while I would never tell you to marry someone, if your heart *is* set on Kevin..."

Briony nodded. She understood. Though as she saw the figure standing forlornly behind the others, she knew that there was one thing she had to do first.

Kailin Gow

Chapter 17

Briony went over to Fallon, taking him by the arm and pulling him back further away from both the fight and the others. She knew that she had to talk this through with him, even though there was nothing he could say that would change anything.

"Briony, don't do this," he said. "You don't have to do this."

Briony shook her head. "I want to do it, Fallon. Yes, marrying Kevin will help us to stop the vampires here and in Wicked, and maybe that's why I'm doing it *now*, but it's not why I'm doing it."

"Then why?" Fallon asked. He looked so hurt in that moment.

"Because I love him," Briony said simply. She knew that would be hard for Fallon to deal with. After all the times she'd bounced back and forth between them, it would be hard on him to find that she'd made a final decision and that it wasn't him, but she had to do it. "I don't know what else to say."

There was one thing she might be able to do to soften the blow though. She couldn't be with him, but there was a chance that she could give him one thing he'd been looking for since he became a vampire. A way back. Hadn't vampires come to Palisor to look for that so many times? If there was a way, then Briony had to believe that the power that would come with marrying Kevin would show her how. She didn't say it right then though. She wanted to be certain before she made a promise like that.

"You're really going to marry Kevin?" Fallon asked. "Even though that will cause all vampires to die."

"I'm going to marry him," Briony confirmed.

"So you're just going to sacrifice me? And Jake? You'll kill your own brother to be happy?"

"The unicorn told me that its horn gave us another way. That the vampires didn't have to die." Briony shook her head. "I would never put Jake at risk like that, Fallon. *Or* you. Not if I thought that marrying Kevin would lead to that. But even Sophie, Josh and the rest seem to agree that it isn't inevitable. It's something we can control. That *I* can control."

Fallon winced. "And there's really nothing that I can do to persuade you to love me?"

"Oh, Fallon," Briony said, reaching out to touch his cheek. "Part of me will always love you. But Kevin... being with him makes me so happy. I'm marrying him."

Fallon nodded. "Then we'd better get on with it. There isn't a lot of time to spare. Once it's dark, the vampires will be nearly unstoppable."

He kissed her then. Softly, obviously saying goodbye.

"Kevin's a lucky guy," Fallon said. He paused. "If you're wrong... if I die, I don't blame you. Just promise you'll remember me."

Fallon didn't give her a chance to answer. Instead he turned and walked away, heading for the heart of the fighting. Briony felt tears washing down her cheeks. She did love Fallon, but she loved Kevin so much more. Enough that even the hurt she felt right then was worth it to be with him. She forced herself to brush away the tears, heading over to Sophie and Vigor.

"How soon can Kevin and I be married?" she asked. She would marry him now or a year from now, but if they couldn't find a way to do it soon, then they would be overwhelmed long before it could happen. How long would it take them to find a church or put together a ceremony? "What do we need to do?"

Vigor gestured to her and Kevin. "Kneel there beside one another. Bow your heads and hold out your hands."

Briony did it, though she started when Vigor drew his sword. The silver steel of it shone bright as the light started to fade over the battlefield. What was he planning to do? There had been a time when she'd been worried that he might try to take the throne. Was he trying that again now? If so, how did he think that Sophie was going to react, standing just behind him?

"Relax," he said. "This is just one of the oldest ceremonies on Palisor. Marriage is a lot of things, and ordinarily we celebrate all of them. For a royal wedding, there would normally be feasting and entertainments, a full week of celebrations. There would be a chance for your subjects to see you and swear their fealty to both you and your new consort. Kevin would be crowned alongside you, your families would take part in the ceremonies, and there would be so much more. Now though, there is no time for all that, and I… well, I suppose I have enough authority to marry you."

"How?" Briony asked.

Vigor smiled. "The most important part is that the two of you are becoming one thing. Do you understand that? Do you want it?"

Briony nodded. Beside her, so did Kevin. She'd barely finished when Vigor took her hand, pressing it to the sword blade. Briony gasped as it drew a line of blood from her palm. Kevin let Vigor do the same with him. The hugtandalfer reached down to tear a strip of white cloth from the padding of his armor. He pressed Briony and Kevin's hands together, tying them loosely with the cloth.

"Briony, do you choose to take Kevin as your husband and consort? Do you promise to love him from now until Palisor is no more?"

Briony didn't have to think about that. "I do."

Vigor turned to Kevin. "Kevin, do you take Briony as your wife and queen? Do *you* promise to love her until Palisor is no more?"

"I do," Kevin said. "I always have."

Vigor nodded and took up his sword once more. He placed it lightly over the cloth binding their hands together, and the fabric parted beneath its edge.

"Cloth can be cut," Vigor said, "but some things are not so easily parted. Briony, Kevin, you are now one whole. Married. Congratulations. And congratulations to you, Briony. Truly, you are the Queen of Palisor now."

"Is this where you say 'you may kiss the bride'?" Sophie asked.

Vigor looked at her. "That is not part of the ceremony."

Briony started to stand, but Kevin cut her off with a kiss.

"I think we'll have to expand it then," Kevin said, when they were done. He helped Briony to her feet. What happened now? She was the queen, but did that mean that she now had all the powers of the scepter? Did she have the power to deal with the vampires in front of her? Just like that? She hoped so, because they were getting closer.

Briony felt the rumbling beneath her feet before she heard it, but once she started to hear it, it was deafening. Hoof beats and running footsteps seemed to come from every direction at once. Briony could hear them, and practically feel them. They were just over…

The gate sprang up without warning, and creatures poured through it. For a second, Vigor and Sophie recoiled, obviously suspecting some kind of surprise attack, but this wasn't that. It was help. Werewolves poured through the gate, and other creatures came with them. Creatures that came straight from the myths of her world. Griffons and giant eagles, trees that walked like people, and people with skin like bark. And unicorns. They came in their hundreds. In their thousands. And at their head was a unicorn with a golden horn, seeming to glow almost ethereally as it strode towards her.

"You?" Briony said. "But I killed you."

"Physically, yes," the unicorn said, the words reverberating out. "But that was necessary. I was the first creature of Palisor, and the first slayer of vampires. I went to fetch my army."

"You were the slayer of vampires?" Briony said. "The vampire apocalypse?"

Unicorns couldn't smile, but Briony suspected it would have if it could. "I was death to them. My horn was. Now, I will be again, if you wish it."

"So the vampires won't all be killed automatically?" Briony asked. She had put her trust in that, but she wanted to be certain now.

"No," the unicorn said. "My horn has much power. Had I lived, it would have heard my will, and my hatred of vampires ran deep. That would have killed them. But I wanted you to have another way. The power to kill, but also the power to change things. And the power to take things from the worlds. Like this army. There are friends of yours here, I think."

Briony looked around, and she saw that she recognized some of the wolves. Jake's small wolf form was easy to pick out. Josh transformed back into his human form, nodding to her gravely. Carol also shifted, though she didn't look happy. Briony hoped she would be, eventually, but Kevin was hers now. Finally, irrevocably hers.

Briony looked around at the battle raging below her on the lowest slopes. Vigor's army was still fighting hard, the dragons using sheets of flame to keep the vampires back for now, but she knew that without help it wouldn't be enough. With the army that stood before her though... she could order the vampires wiped out so easily.

Briony shook her head. She wasn't going to do that. There were better ways. Ways that didn't involve that kind of killing. She turned to the unicorn.

"I just want them gone," she said. "Driven back to Xylyx and buried again. There are too many vampires I care about to let you kill them all."

The unicorn said, "And that is why I let you slay me. Very well, it will be as you ask. One final thing. Have you ever wondered why the scepter is *called* a scepter?"

Briony had wondered that a couple of times. It was only a large pendant really. Something that she could wear around her neck on a chain. She'd assumed before that it had been a scepter once, but that the handle had rotted or been destroyed. In that moment though, she understood.

She lifted the golden horn of the unicorn that she had been fighting with and took the scepter from around her neck. She could feel them both thrumming with power, the way they had back in her room. She pressed the two together.

There was a flash of power, and Briony was surprised to feel it flowing through *her*. It was Palisor. The power of the land. The people. The *life*. And in that moment she was all of it. That power poured into the scepter, and it *was* a scepter now, only it was so much more than that. As Briony watched, it lengthened, becoming a staff as tall as her shoulder. A staff that shone golden with power.

Briony lifted it, and that power flashed out as golden light, brighter than the setting sun by far. Where it touched the darkness that flowed along with the vampires, that darkness dissolved, leaving the savage vampires there blinking in the light and even shrinking back from the sheer force of it. In that moment, Briony understood how her father had managed to drive the creatures back.

"Let's go send these things back to their prison," she yelled, charging forward. The unicorn's army charged with her, but that wasn't the most important thing. The most important thing was Kevin, in wolf form now and loping steadily by her side. Her husband. Her consort. Her love.

Chapter 18

Briony led the charge, the knowledge of everything she had to do next pounding in her ears as loudly as her blood was right then. Sophie and Valor, Josh, Jake and all the others ran with her, people she cared about mixed in with the horde of fantastic creatures there to fight against the vampires. And at the heart of them, right next to her, was Kevin. Her husband.

Just those words were so strange. Strange, but beautiful too. And right, like Briony had always known them. Maybe she had. Despite everything she'd felt for anyone else, despite Fallon, she'd kept coming back to Kevin. Now he was hers, and she was his. She thought about the vampires ahead of them. She was *not* going to let them do anything to ruin their happiness.

Briony had the completed scepter in her hand, and she could feel the power within it. She ran with it like a spear, somehow knowing that it was the weapon she needed. The weapon they all needed. However far Xylyx was, they were going to force these creatures back into it. They were getting close now, and ahead of them hugtandalfer warriors fought and died, the inhuman sounds of the vampires mingling with the battle cries of the soldiers. The vampires seemed somehow less organized now, with their shrouding darkness banished. They still attacked ferociously, but they did so individually, not swarming the hugtandalfer warriors in mad mobs.

The lines clashed, and for a moment or two, everything was chaos. A vampire lunged at Kevin, and instinctively, Briony thrust the scepter into the creature's path to block it. The vampire barely brushed the golden staff, but power burst within it, leaving nothing but ashes where it had stood. Briony stared openmouthed at what had just happened. She'd known that the scepter had power. She'd known that it was a weapon, but this…

She'd spent the last few months trying to strike at vampires' hearts. That was part of what made them so deadly, because to kill them, you had to come almost within their embrace. If this staff could kill them with just a touch though… Briony swung it experimentally, catching another of the vampires on the leg. Again, there was a flash of golden light, and the creature was simply gone.

Kevin leapt in after her, biting wherever he could. Briony saw the other werewolves doing the same. Jake seemed almost to be making a game out of it, darting between the legs of the vampires trying to kill them all, nipping and biting where he could. It seemed simply playful, except that every time he bit, a vampire died. Every time any of the werewolves bit, vampires died.

Archer and the other dragons flew above them, safer now that they had more support. With the werewolves cannoning into the fight on the ground, several of the hugtandalfer fighters were able to step back and nock bows, using them to target any creatures that tried to jump up to bring the dragons to the ground. That left the dragons free to burn.

Briony almost reeled back as the first gouts of flame struck the ground, seemingly just yards from her. Close enough at least that she could feel the heat from them. Archer burned a line of flame along the flank of the vampire forces, scything down those creatures that fell within the flames, while Fletcher flew on the other side of them, doing the same. For a moment or two, Briony didn't understand what the dragons were doing, but then she saw it. They were containing the vampires, stopping them from spreading out around their forces and coming in from the flanks.

Stopping them from getting away that way too, because then the unicorns and other creatures of Palisor hit them. Briony had been a little worried about that part. Unicorns were beautiful, but she couldn't see how they could be deadly. These were though. Some struck vampires and trampled them, knocking them down so that werewolves had easy bites. Some tore at them with their teeth and pummeled them with their hooves. More used their horns, piercing the vampires and in some cases killing them outright when they struck them through the heart. With their size and weight, the unicorns were even able to attack some of the strange, chitin covered creatures that skittered along with the vampires, cracking them open or squashing them like bugs. Griffons clawed at them, while eagles intercepted those that could fly as they tried to get away.

The battle grew more hectic then, and for a moment or two, Briony could concentrate on nothing but the fights immediately around her. She spun the scepter like a baton, keeping it moving, knowing that wherever it struck an enemy it would be enough. She twirled it in figure of eights, making after images blur through the air as it struck vampire after withered vampire. One of the hard shelled creatures with them came forward at her and Briony brought the scepter down on it with an audible crack. Sophie leapt at it, finishing it, while Vigor spun in behind her, fending off a vampire who charged at her back. Sophie smiled at him then in a way Briony had never seen her great aunt smile at anyone else.

The vampires kept coming. Would they have to kill them all to stop them? No. Briony was sure of that. Her father had driven them back, and so would she. Without the darkness binding them together as it had, they lacked the purpose they had possessed before. They were throwing themselves forward out of wild, animal fury, but even animals could be made to run when they weren't bound together by whatever power had been connecting them.

Briony swung her staff left and right, and everywhere it touched, vampires died. Another leapt at Kevin, and she stopped it with a touch. One swung claws at Sophie, and Briony took its legs from under it with her foot before bringing the staff down. Kevin stayed by her, protecting her back, making sure that no vampires could get to her before the whirling sweep of the staff could get to them. Around her, the werewolves bit, the unicorns skewered, and the dragons rained down fire, so that the battle was as hot as an oven.

Even so the fight wasn't all one way. Briony saw a werewolf she didn't know killed from behind by a vampire that leapt upon it and started rending it with its claws. The werewolf twisted enough to bite it, but by then, the damage was done. Half trained Hugtandalfer warriors fell as they tried to match the efforts of the werewolves, or of their queen. A unicorn collapsed with its throat torn out, in a sight that was uncomfortably close to the way the first unicorn had looked after she had killed it.

Slowly though, so slowly that at first she didn't notice it, Briony could feel the tide of the battle turning. Vampires were slower to throw themselves forward now as she attacked, and there seemed to be less of a storm of claws and teeth around the edges of her vision. She saw Sophie actually standing there with nothing to fight for a second or two, when previously her great aunt had been at the heart of the action. The werewolves were still busy biting any vampires they could get close to, but more and more of them were shying away from them.

Briony charged forward at another knot of vampires. They looked at her for a second or so, and then seemed to make a decision. Or maybe it wasn't as calculated as that. Maybe it was just their primal instinct for self-preservation. Either way, before Briony could reach them with the staff, they turned and they ran. That was the tipping point. Briony could sense it. She pressed forward, and the werewolves surged with her.

Like birds startled from their perches by the flight of one of their number, the vampires turned and sprinted down the mountain path. Those that didn't died. When they were coming forward, the vampires were a deadly wave of violence without thought, but that also meant that once they started to panic, they couldn't stop themselves. They fled, while Briony and the wolves ran after them.

It would have been so easy to stand there and let them run, but Briony knew that this needed to be finished. Palisor needed to be safe. Briony summoned her magic, sending a burst of fire after the running vampires, then lifted her face to the sky.

"Archer!"

The dragon was there like he'd been waiting for her summons. He dropped to earth, letting Briony climb aboard his back before taking to the air again and sending flames to match hers into the ranks of the vampires. The few who weren't already in retreat routed then. The wolves, the dragons and the unicorns kept after them, leaving behind those hugtandalfers who were too slow to keep up. Though Briony saw that Fletcher had acquired two familiar silver clad passengers. It seemed that Sophie and Vigor weren't going to miss the hunt.

From this height, she could see the point of the burning along the edges of the vampire horde the dragons had done. Flames still licked at those edges, and whenever it looked like vampires might break away to one side or the other, dragons swooped low to add their fire to them. They were funneling the vampires down the path, controlling the route they took as they fled before the rest of Briony's army.

How long did the chase take? Longer than any human army could have sustained it, that was for certain. The vampires ran and ran, the chasing werewolves not letting them slow. They hunted the vampires across mile after mile, forcing them back over rocky ground, always in the same direction.

Briony felt it before she saw it. A scar on the landscape that she felt as though it were part of her. A long, jagged split around which vampires and other creatures thronged, seeming to roil like a dark tide. Briony held out the staff she held, and light sprang from it, illuminating them, almost seeming to push at them as they shrank back before that power. Some of them fled then, heading back into the welcoming depths of the chasm. Others turned tail when they saw the rest of their horde running towards them, driven on by the wolves and unicorns.

A few needed the dragons' flames, Archer and his family opening up in concert to blast those who refused to flee with white hot fire. The vampires screamed and scrambled for cover in the only place they felt safe. Xylyx.

Those fleeing the werewolves followed them, a great, screaming horde that plunged into the chasm, apparently unconcerned about how many of their number fell over the edge to crash into the depths so long as *they* could get away from the wolves. They ran, until minutes after Xylyx had come into sight, the last of them disappeared into its depths.

Archer took Briony down then, so that she dismounted in the middle of her army of werewolves and unicorns. She stood there, and they seemed to be watching for her cue. If she told them to go into Xylyx and kill all they found there, she knew that they would. But there was another way. Briony could feel it as surely as, right then, she could feel the land around her. The opening to Xylyx might look like a natural feature, but it was a portal, the same as the ways to Wicked were portals.

And now, Briony knew that the portals would answer to her. Archer shifted beside her, adopting his human form and putting a hand on Briony's shoulder. A wolf ran forward from the hunting pack, so that a second later, Kevin was standing beside her, his hand in hers. Briony held the scepter, complete with all the power of Palisor. She said only one word.

"Close."

The chasm shuddered, the earth around it shaking so that the wolves around it howled in discomfort and moved away from the edge. Briony, Kevin and Archer stood still. Gradually, with the rumble of moving rock, the edges of the chasm moved closer together. They ground closer and closer, the sheer weight of rock moving just with Briony's power so great that she knew if she thought about it, she wouldn't be able to do it. Yet she was queen, and she *could* do it. This was her kingdom. It obeyed her.

The edges of the chasm met with a final, resounding crash. Xylyx was closed.

Chapter 19

It took a minute or two for Sophie and Vigor to land and join Briony. By that time, a lot of the werewolves had transformed back into their human shapes. Some were celebrating, while others were staring around at Palisor like they couldn't quite believe it was real. Josh was there with his sister, making his way through the crowd of magical creatures towards them. Jake was there too, and Briony could see Fallon near him, looking very nervous at the heart of a crowd of creatures that had so recently been killing every vampire they could find. He didn't need to worry though, Briony wasn't going to let anyone hurt either him or her brother.

Ahead of them, Xylyx was closed. There was a faint scar on the landscape; a gouge of uprooted trees and displaced earth, but Briony knew that would quickly become overgrown. In a year, or maybe just a few months, it would be like Xylyx had never been there. Yet it was.

Briony knew that too. She had dealt with the threat, but she was the queen here. She had to go *on* dealing with anything that threatened Palisor.

Beside her, Kevin transformed back into his human self. His clothing was badly torn, but Briony didn't mind that. Now that they were married, she planned on seeing a lot more than just a few flashes of muscle glimpsed through half ruined clothes. She put an arm around him, enjoying the moment.

"It is over, your majesty," Vigor said, striding forward and bowing deeply. "May I be the first to congratulate you on your victory?"

Beside him, Sophie rolled her eyes. "You can tell he grew up in a royal court, can't you? Straighten up, Vigor. You'll embarrass my great-niece, even if this angle is giving me a nice view."

Vigor straightened up so fast, it was like something had bitten him. Sophie laughed. Somehow, Briony got the feeling that in the aftermath of all this, the two of them would be spending a lot more time together.

"This isn't over, Briony." Josh stepped forward, looking at her seriously.

Vigor turned to him, obviously glad for the change of topic. "What do you mean, Werewolf King? We have won the day. The vampires that threatened Palisor are gone. Briony has come into her full power as queen. It is done. It is *over*."

Josh shook his head, looking pointedly at Briony. "You know what I mean. This isn't done."

Vigor bristled at that. "I insist-"

"He's right, Vigor," Sophie said. She looked over to Briony. "There's still a lot to do. Not here maybe, but it still needs doing. Palisor might be safe, but there's still Wicked to think about."

Briony nodded. They were right. This wasn't done. She'd seen some of what was happening in the reflecting pool. Pietre was there, and the town was in trouble.

"I know," she said. She looked around at the werewolves, the unicorns, and the other creatures that had joined her in the fight against the vampires. She lifted the scepter, and in that instant, all eyes were on her. "Listen to me, all of you. You've done great things here today, but we aren't done. Many of you don't belong in Palisor, and I need to get you home, but it is likely that there is another fight waiting for us there. Are you ready for that fight?"

The roar that greeted those words was almost deafening. Briony looked across to Archer.

"Are you ready?"

The dragon nodded. Briony understood this part now. She'd done it once before, by reflex, but she hadn't been able to control it. Now, with the full power of Palisor behind her, she could *feel* how it worked, and where the dragons came into it. The link with them was a focus. A key. She could summon the gates, but Archer's natural talent made it easy to unlock them.

Briony focused and thought of Wicked. She summoned up power, and while she held the scepter, she could feel that it didn't come *through* the scepter. It was her power. The power that came with being the queen of this place. She just had to use it. She extended her closed hand in front of her, and slowly, carefully, opened it.

Mist sprang up, shifting and billowing as it flowed upwards into the familiar shape of an arch. With Archer so close, Briony could feel the mist within it pulsing and stretching like the skin of a drum, or perhaps like the surface tension of a lake. She concentrated, making sure that she pictured Wicked in every detail on the other side. She didn't know if that would help or not, but how else was she meant to make sure that the gate came out where she wanted?

Archer stepped forward, and the gate sprang into life, the mist within it clearing as the dragon took a step through it. Briony realized what she'd done as that happened, because she could see George's diner there, the people clustered within it. She'd been so busy simply thinking about Wicked that she hadn't thought *where* in Wicked she should open the gate. It looked like she'd done it right in the middle of town. Well, it was too late to do much about that.

"Everyone who's coming to Wicked, go through the gate now," she commanded, and even though she knew that she was the queen, it was still slightly surprising to see so many people jumping to obey her. The werewolves poured back through, though Josh paused before he did so.

"Will my people be able to come back here?"

Briony nodded. "The restrictions are gone. I don't plan on putting them back in place. There needs to be somewhere your kind can live openly."

"Good," Josh said, heading through. Carol glanced back at her, or maybe at Kevin, before stepping through. Sophie stepped through after them, still dressed in her armor. To Briony's surprise, Vigor stepped through after her. Jake jumped through along with them, and Fallon slipped through in the same moment. Finally, it was her turn. She looked over at Kevin, took his hand, and stepped through.

They were, as the image through the gate had suggested, right outside George's diner. Through the windows, Briony could see people staring at them. Several members of the Preservation Society had weapons out, like they were convinced that this was some new threat to deal with. There were so many people in there, and just one glance at the diner told Briony it had come under attack. One of the windows was broken, while there were gouges in the brickwork outside.

"It's all right. It's Briony." Maisy came out from inside, dragging Steve in her wake. George stepped out with them, obviously looking a little concerned. At least until he saw Sophie.

"Sophie Edge? Is that you? What *happened*?"

"It's a long story, George," Sophie said, moving off with him with the obvious intention of telling him all of it. Vigor looked to Briony, like he knew he ought to stay with her.

"Go with Sophie," Briony commanded, and Vigor went with her. Briony could hear her great-aunt explaining some of what had happened to George and the rest of the Preservation Society, but she knew that Maisy would have her own questions.

"Why is there a portal in the middle of town?" her friend asked. "What's with all the werewolves? Why are you carrying that staff? And that ring… that's Kevin's ring, isn't it?"

"Slow down," Briony said, holding up her hands. "That's a lot of questions to have to answer at once. A lot's happened very quickly. Come inside, and I'll try to explain."

They headed back inside. Jake and Fallon were sitting with Sophie, Vigor and George. The rest of the

Preservation Society was crowded around, listening to Sophie's account of what had happened. Briony knew that she should fill Maisy and Steve in on the key parts, but right then, there were things she needed to know more than she needed to tell them.

"What happened here?" Briony asked.

"Pietre," Steve supplied. "He's been launching attacks more or less constantly for at least a day. He attacks us here, then while we're pinned here, he has his vampires grab people from the town and transform them. It's crazy."

"Like he thinks it's the end of the world or something," Maisy put in. "We've all heard him talking about some kind of vampire apocalypse. It's like he thinks if he has enough vampires, he'll be able to avoid it."

"Or maybe he just wants to take more people with him," Steve suggested.

Briony didn't know what to say to that. She'd stopped the vampire apocalypse. By killing the first unicorn of Palisor and taking its horn, she'd put herself in a position to prevent it. To deal with the vampires another way.

"It's good to have you back," Maisy said. She looked at Briony's finger, then at her face, then at Kevin. "Isn't that Kevin's ring? Are you two…"

"We're married," Briony said.

"Married!" Maisy put a hand over her mouth and practically jumped for joy. Then she hugged Briony so tightly Briony thought that she might be crushed. Maisy stepped back from her, looking stern. "And you didn't invite me?"

"We *were* in another world," Briony pointed out.

"Like that's an…"

Maisy tailed off. Silence crept over the diner. Briony looked outside and saw why instantly. Pietre stood in the middle of the street. He had vampires with him. Dozens of them. More. They thronged in front of the diner, looking almost strange after the vampires of Xylyx. At least those had looked like monsters. These… for the most part they looked like kids. Confused kids, with the occasional adult here and there where the vampires had been able to grab them. Briony recognized at least a couple of members of the town's council.

Pietre stood there staring at the gate to Palisor until Briony sent out a whisper of power to close it. She stepped out into the street with Kevin and Fallon on one side of her, Sophie and Vigor moving to the other. Around her, Briony could see werewolves positioning themselves for a fight. Astonishingly, this might be a harder fight than against the vampires from the chasm, because here, werewolves didn't retain the deadliness of their bite the way they did in Palisor.

Pietre ignored Briony, looking at Sophie. Staring at her like he'd never seen her before like this. Briony knew he had. He'd been involved in too many of the fights with Marcus not to have noticed her transformation. Yet, put like that, he'd probably never had a chance to really stop and appreciate the change.

"I can't get used to you looking like that, Sophie," he said. "You're... *you* again. The same girl who loved me so much. The same girl who *betrayed* me."

"You keep using that as an excuse, Pietre," Sophie said. She drew her swords. Beside her, Vigor did the same. "You've been busy. Killing people. Forcing them to be what you are."

"I'll do whatever I need to do to survive," Pietre said. "I'll turn every one of you if I have to."

"No you won't," Briony said, stepping forward.

Pietre turned to her. "Quiet girl, I'm talking to your aunt."

Briony brought her staff down sharply on the sidewalk. It let out a quick burst of light that made Pietre take a step back.

"What-" the master vampire managed.

"You'll talk to me," Briony said. "At least if you want to live."

Chapter 20

Pietre stood there at the head of his vampires, staring at Briony. He had so many vampires with him now, but Briony found that for once, she wasn't afraid. Not even after everything he'd done to her and her family. She wasn't even angry anymore. Pietre wasn't worth her anger. He simply had to be stopped.

"You've grown in power," Pietre observed. "You're very different from the frightened little girl who showed up in town to stay with her great aunt."

"I've changed," Briony said. "We all have. You haven't. I'm the Queen of Palisor now, Aunt Sophie is the hugtandalfer she was always meant to be, Fallon and Kevin have come into their powers, even Maisy and Steve have had to live through a lot. But you... all this, and you're still trying to do the same things you were at the start."

"I'm a vampire," Pietre sneered. "We aren't meant to change. We are eternal, there when you and all your kind have gone. Ten thousand years from now, I will still be here."

Briony thought of the vampires from Xylyx, each unimaginably ancient. Each utterly mindless and animal. Perhaps they had always been like that, but maybe time had done it to them too. So much time that they could never be anything else except insane.

"Be careful what you wish for," Briony said softly. She felt Kevin move up beside her.

Pietre looked at them oddly. "The werewolf won out then? And is that a ring I see on your finger, Briony? You're... married?"

Briony nodded. "I'm married, and I'm the queen of Palisor. *Fully* the queen. Where did you think the gate came from?"

Pietre stared at her. "But that... that's *impossible*."

"Why?"

"Because if you are the queen, then the apocalypse... we should be dead! I have spent *days* trying to find enough vampires to resist it. Are you saying that I *succeeded*?"

He hadn't been sure. All that time he'd spent transforming innocent kids into his kind, and he hadn't even been sure it would work. However much Pietre liked to play the part of the cunning master vampire, in his heart, he'd just been a scared, desperate creature trying to cling onto any hope of life, regardless of what that cost anyone else. Maybe he always had been.

"You didn't succeed," Briony assured him.

"I am still here, aren't I? My power is-"

"Your power is nothing," Sophie said, stepping forward as though she might attack. "You're still alive because Briony is a better person than you will ever be. She took her power, and she controlled it. She has more compassion, and more love, in her than you will ever have. *She* stopped the destruction of the vampires, Pietre, not you."

Pietre shook his head. "No, that can't be. I have seen the power of the vampires on Palisor. I have *felt* some of what was rising up. I know the legends. The only way you could beat them would be to unleash that power."

"You're still alive, aren't you?" Briony pointed out.

"Briony followed her father's path," Sophie explained. "She drove them back. She locked them away. The way we're going to lock you away, Pietre."

Pietre laughed then. "You don't have the power. None of you do. Again and again, you've tried to destroy me. Again and again, you have failed. I survived the vampire apocalypse through *my* power, and so did my vampires."

Briony saw then just how mad the master vampire was. How mad he'd always been. Yet he could still think. Still choose. In his way, he was worse than the Xylyx vampires had been. Worse even than Marcus had been. The vampires from the chasm had been nothing more than killing machines, while Marcus… as evil as he had been, he'd really been nothing more than the product of a time when the world had been more brutal.

Pietre didn't have those excuses. He was old, but not so old that he didn't understand how the world worked. He'd claimed to love Sophie once, yet he'd killed so many members of her and Briony's family. He'd terrorized Wicked. He'd gone to war with the werewolves and tried to force her to give him a way into Palisor. He'd tried to manipulate Marcus, controlled half of the town's council and now it seemed that he was determined to transform everyone he could into his kind.

It was time for that to stop. Whatever it took.

"Pietre," Briony said. "I gave Marcus a chance. I told him that he could live. Well, I'm going to make you an offer that's better than that. Humanity. I don't know how to do it yet, but I believe that the scepter has the power to make you human again. Surrender, and I will try to give you that."

Pietre looked at her incredulously. "Do you think I *want* that?" He gestured to his unremarkable, middle aged form. "Do you think I want to age any more than I have? Do you think I want to grow old and die? Remind me, how long do the hugtandalfer live?"

A long time. Briony hadn't thought about that much yet, but she had a long life ahead of her as Palisor's queen. At least assuming nothing went wrong in the next few minutes.

"And if you could actually do it," Pietre pointed out, "you'd have transformed young Fallon already. We all know how much he aches to be human again."

"I haven't done it yet," Briony admitted, "but I'm sure that I can."

"And all I have to do is surrender?" Pietre laughed at that. He turned to the vampires he'd transformed, and to the older ones with them. "Kill them. Kill all of them. This ends here."

The vampires rushed forward. If they'd still been in Palisor, it wouldn't have been close to an even fight. The werewolves would have been able to kill the vampires far too easily for that. Yet here, where they didn't have the same deadliness in their bite, it was a different story.

Briony felt water falling around her, and she saw that sprinklers had started around the diner. She saw the holy water in them burn a couple of vampires who came too close, but for the most part the fight was away from the diner. Away from the diner, but in the middle of the street. What would the people of Wicked think about vampires and werewolves battling through their town? About the same things they'd thought about being dragged away to be transformed into vampires, probably. The town was never going to be the same.

For now though, Briony had more immediate things to think about. A vampire leapt at her, screaming in rage. She hit it with the staff she carried and it burst into flames. She spun, summoning up her magic and blasting another with fire. Archer, obviously taking his cue from her, transformed and strafed more vampires with flame. More than a few of the new vampires looked at the dragon in terror.

The werewolves rushed forward, working as a pack. Josh hit a vampire low, so that Carol could tear his throat out. Jake ripped another to pieces, while Kevin kept his human form and slipped behind one who came at him, breaking the vampire's neck. It was fast and brutal, a sudden wave of violence that was somehow worse because it was happening here. Huge battles with magical creatures involved were chaotic and terrifying on Palisor, but at least they fit there. Here, they were just *wrong*.

Briony saw Sophie going after Pietre. She should have known that her great aunt would do that, and so far, she seemed to be making a good job of it. She was cutting her way through the crowd of new vampires, her swords swinging in glittering arcs. Even the older vampires that were left from Pietre's group barely slowed her down, and if they did, it was only long enough that Vigor could appear by her side to lend his blade to the assault.

Briony stepped forward into the fight, swinging the staff she held. Killing vampires. She saw that Sophie had cornered Pietre now, and the master vampire's claws skittered against her blades, drawing sparks as though they were also made of steel. Pietre disappeared from in front of her, winding shadows around himself, and a second later Sophie cried out as a line of blood appeared on her leg. She managed to get a swift sword thrust in though, forcing Pietre back.

The Preservation Society had joined the fight by then, their weapons adding stakes and crossbow bolts, vials of holy water and silver blades to the battle. Briony saw Maisy fire a crossbow at a vampire to get the attention of a whole group of them, only for Steve to throw a water bomb as they got closer. Briony spun then, moving to intercept another vampire as it tried to get close to her…

…and found herself face to face with Pepper Freeman. Briony hadn't thought too much about the other kids at Wicked's high school in the past month or two.

She'd spent her time fighting wars they couldn't understand, in places they wouldn't believe existed. She doubted that most of them would even remember her, given how little time she was there. Yet she remembered Pepper. After all, the head cheerleader had gone out of her way to make life unpleasant for her. Now here she was, her mouth open to reveal fangs. When had they transformed her? Had she just been walking down the wrong street? Had she volunteered? After all, her family had always supported Pietre.

She was here. She was a vampire, and just the slightest touch of the scepter would be enough to destroy her. Briony kicked her away instead, back into the melee. She couldn't do it. She might have thought she hated Pepper once, but after all this? Pepper didn't matter. She was just some kid who used to be mean to her. Set against everything else Briony had come up against, she wasn't important, except as a reminder that these *weren't* faceless, mindless beasts they were killing.

Briony slammed the staff on the ground again, sending out another wave of painfully bright light.

"Stop! Everybody *stop!*"

Briony poured as much of her power into those words as she could, and almost to her amazement, they worked. Fights ground to a halt in front of her. Vampires looked around like they couldn't quite remember what they were doing. Briony concentrated, forcing her magic into whatever space Pietre's control over them occupied. If she could do it with the Xylyx vampires, she could do it with these.

Slowly, impossibly, the battle ground to a halt. It was obvious that the vampires were losing. Most of the older ones were dead.

"Stop," Briony said.

"Ignore her," Pietre countered, stepping forward. "*Kill* her."

"Why do you have to do what Pietre says?" Briony demanded. She kept her magic pulsing out. "He's just a foolish old man who has lived too long. If you fight, you'll probably end up dead. You can see how the fight has been going."

"I *command* you to kill her!" Pietre raged, grabbing a vampire and shoving him towards Briony. He struck the scepter and disintegrated.

"That's what he'll do with you," Briony said. "He'll use you up and throw you away. He doesn't care about you. He doesn't deserve to lead you. You *don't* have to do what he says."

There was a murmur from the vampires. While she was able to hold Pietre's control in check, they could obviously think for themselves. At least, some of them started to drift away from the edges of the fight. Pietre looked at them in fury.

"No," he said. "*No*. You'll die for this. You'll all die. And *you...*" he turned his attention back to Briony, his eyes flaring red. He started forward and Briony raised the scepter. But there was no need for it, because in that moment a second shape hit Pietre from the side.

Fallon.

Chapter 21

Fallon hit Pietre so hard in that first clash that Briony winced. She started to move forward to help, but she knew that she couldn't. Not yet. People had only stopped fighting because of her. If she started again, then things would go very wrong, very quickly. So she had to stand there while Fallon jumped at Pietre, lashing out at him with fists and feet while the master vampire came back at him with claws.

When had Fallon gotten fast enough to dodge those sweeping nails? When had he acquired the strength to hold Pietre back as the master vampire tried to thrust his fangs forward into Fallon's throat?

"You can't beat me boy," Pietre said. "You're still young. *I* am a master vampire."

"The only thing you're a master of," Fallon shot back, kicking him hard in the stomach, "is talking too much."

Pietre stumbled back, and then seemed to recover. He lunged at Fallon, and those claws of his drew blood. "I made you. Everything you are today is because of me."

For a moment, Fallon had to give ground as Pietre attacked, the master vampire's hands moving in patterns too fast for the eye to follow.

"Everything I am today comes from not being what *you* are," Fallon retorted. He kicked down, catching Pietre in the knee hard enough that the master vampire cried out. "It comes from having people around me who care about me. People I love." He glanced back at Briony then.

"And look what has happened," Pietre argued. "She married your brother. A werewolf. She betrayed you, the way Sophie betrayed me. We should be on the same side."

He lunged then, tackling Fallon to the ground and rearing over him. He hit Fallon once, then again.

"Look at you. You're pathetic. You go on about love, but you don't even have it anymore. What's left after that? Love is a lie."

Fallon shoved up, pushing Pietre off him.

"You're wrong, Pietre."

He hit the master vampire hard in the stomach, moving to dodge the swipe of his fingernails.

"Briony might have married Kevin, but that doesn't change how beautiful loving her was. It doesn't change the fact that loving her kept me from being like you. It doesn't change how much I care about my friends, about my brother, about everyone who still cares about me."

He hit Pietre again and again.

"You've gained a lot of power in your trips to Palisor," Pietre said. "But I have my own tricks."

He started to weave shadows around himself, but Fallon darted forward, grabbing at the spot where he'd started to disappear. He didn't seem to care about the wounds that appeared almost all over him.

"It wasn't Palisor," Fallon said. "It was just realizing that I *was* strong. It was having people around me who wanted me to be strong. That's not what you are, Pietre. You pretend to be strong, and to do that, you keep the people around you weak. Well, I'm not weak. Let me show you."

Fallon leapt the way only he could leap, and he carried Pietre with him. Together they rose into the air so high that even Briony could barely make them out. Then they dropped. They dropped together like a stone. Faster than Fallon normally fell. Faster than could be safe, even for a vampire. Briony saw Pietre then, struggling underneath Fallon as the younger vampire drove him down into the ground like a hammer.

They hit the concrete with a crash hard enough to crack the sidewalk. Dust flew up, making it impossible to see what was happening. All Briony could do was stand there, and hope, and maybe feel a little guilty for hoping.

"It's okay," Kevin said beside her, slipping his hand into hers. "I hope he's all right too."

The dust cleared, and Fallon was standing there. Pietre was at his feet, looking up and groaning. The master vampire looked like he could barely move then, but Briony knew even that wouldn't be enough. Eventually, he would heal. Eventually, he would try to cause more chaos in Wicked. A month ago, she would have staked him. Now though, she had another option.

She looked over to Archer, who was back in his human shape. "Xylyx isn't the only pocket of reality connected to Palisor, is it?"

"No, my queen."

"Are there any that would hold a vampire?"

"Several."

Briony nodded and let go of Kevin's hand so that she could touch her fingers to Archer's shoulder. "Think of one."

Before, she had thought of the location the gate would open to. She'd been the one thinking of Wicked, trying to get home. Now, she just summoned her power, trusting that Archer would find the right place for this gate to open. Briony stared at the patch of ground beneath Pietre, pulling magic into her. Then she released it.

The sidewalk where Pietre lay seemed to swirl like a whirlpool, going from something solid to something so fluid the vampire slid through without a sound. There *were* sounds though, on the other side. The sound of hounds barking and steel doors slamming closed. The sound of marching feet and people shouting things a long way off. An image came into Briony's mind of a dungeon. Of a world that was nothing *but* dungeons. Mile upon mile of underground imprisonment. Somewhere even Pietre would have trouble escaping from. Briony let the power fade and the sidewalk went back to being just a sidewalk.

She looked around. There were so many people in the street. There were vampires there, members of the Preservation Society, and werewolves. There were ordinary people from the town, who looked around as though knowing that their lives would never be the same again. Wicked had always been the town where people managed to ignore the supernatural things happening around them, yet now, Briony suspected that wasn't going to be possible anymore.

Fallon looked bad right then. He had several deep wounds, yet he seemed to be ignoring them for the moment. He looked around the assembled crowd, staring at the vampires there.

"Most of you don't know what is going on," he said. "You were turned without a choice and pushed by Pietre to feed your hunger by hurting people. It doesn't have to be that way. You have a choice, and you need to make it, if you aren't going to be the kind of monster who gets hunted down. Think of your friends, your families. The people who love you."

"And then what?" Pepper asked it. Briony was almost glad to see that she'd survived the fight.

"And then you keep on doing it," Fallon told her. He looked around again. "How many of you are there now? Too many to go around hunting people. *One* vampire is too many to have hunting people. We'll have to find a new way. A better way. And we will. Come on, all of you. We should leave. There are a lot of things we need to talk about."

He led the way, and the vampires followed him. Briony wasn't surprised by that. Right then, they were looking for someone to help them make sense of things. Had any of Pietre's older vampires survived? She couldn't see any of them, and they would have been at the heart of the fighting. Even if they had, Pietre wasn't there anymore to command them. Maybe they would change. So long as Fallon kept control of the rest, maybe it didn't matter whether they did or not.

"You're just going to let them go?" Josh asked. "You think that vampires can live without hunting down humans?"

"Do you want another fight that badly, Josh?" Briony countered. "It's done. Maybe it isn't done forever, but life doesn't work like that. For now, we just have to find a way to make things work."

The first thing that meant was getting everyone off the street. That took a while. Most of the werewolves wouldn't leave until Josh ordered them. Then there were the members of the Preservation Society, who were reluctant to move out from the safety of George's Diner until they were certain that this wasn't all some ploy by the vampires to get them into the open. There were plenty of ordinary people in there too, sheltering away from Pietre and his creatures. Most of them looked like they'd seen far too much in a short space of time.

In the end, they decided to make George's Diner their base while they talked through what would happen next. Josh showed up again with his sister, while Fallon came in with a couple of people Briony recognized as members of the town's council. Briony knew that she ought to be at the heart of what happened next, but at the start of it at least there were so many people trying to talk at once that she just wanted to take a step back. She commandeered a booth with Kevin and just sat there with him, content to let the rest of it was over her while she waited for the arguments to subside a little. Somewhere along the line, she must have drifted off to sleep, because she found herself waking with her head on Kevin's shoulder.

Briony smiled at the thought that she might be doing that for a long time to come. Then she looked up and saw why she'd woken up. Sophie was there, sitting down opposite them.

"What did I miss?" Briony asked.

"A bit," Sophie admitted. "Josh and Fallon spent a while arguing over what should happen to the vampires next, but Josh has his own problems. His pack doesn't want any more fighting."

"So what's going to happen?" Briony asked.

Sophie shrugged. "Pietre's lieutenants seem to be either dead or gone. Fallon's the oldest vampire left, and all the kids who were turned… well, they remember him from school. I think if anybody can teach them not to kill humans, it's him."

"Will that work?" Kevin asked.

"It worked for George." Sophie looked over to the diner's owner. "Who is now *Councilman* George, incidentally."

"How did that happen?" Briony asked. "I mean, people can't just *decide* that you're going to be on the town's council."

"Ordinarily, no," Sophie said, "but the circumstances are pretty special now. We have a town where people have just found out that they're going to have to live alongside the supernatural. We have a large vampire population, one that's mostly made up of people's kids. It needs people on the council with the experience to cope with the situation."

"So George got a job?" Briony finished.

Sophie smiled. "Not just George. There are a lot of vacancies now all the council representatives who supported Pietre have been persuaded to resign."

"When did that happen?" Kevin asked.

Sophie looked at her watch. "Oh, I think Vigor will be getting around to the last of them about now. Would *you* want to hold onto a seat if you'd been helping vampires? After everything Pietre has done?"

"So who else is on the council?"

"Most of the Preservation Society," Sophie said. She looked slightly uncomfortable. "And me. I couldn't find a way to talk myself out of it."

Briony found herself thinking of the way Sophie was around Vigor. She couldn't imagine Vigor staying in this world, yet Sophie would need to if she was going to attend council meetings.

"I can commute," Sophie said as though guessing Briony's thoughts. "It just so happens that my great-niece is very good at making gateways." Sophie smiled. "You're going to need to be."

Briony hadn't thought of that. There was so much to do here, but Palisor was hers now. Hers and Kevin's. They'd have to go back and forth a lot.

"It sounds like there's a lot to do," Briony observed.

Sophie nodded. "Yes. But some of them will be more fun than others."

Epilogue

They held the wedding in the cloud palace, with row after row of guests stretched out across the great hall. Briony stood in front of the thrones at the head of the hall with Kevin. She wore a dress of silver and white fabric that seemed to shimmer with every breath she took. She said the two words she'd wanted to say ever since Sophie and the others suggested doing this over.

"I do."

The crowd cheered, and there were enough people there that for a moment or two it was deafening. Maisy, Steve and the rest of the Preservation Society were there, looking around like they couldn't quite believe the place they'd walked into. Archer, Fletcher and the rest of the dragons were on balconies around the place. As Briony said those two beautiful words they leapt off, transforming and breathing fire in a kind of aerial salute. Josh, the werewolves, hugtandalfer folk from a hundred different parts of her kingdom... they were all there to watch her marry Kevin. They didn't seem to care that they were already married. For royalty, it was the show that counted.

The hugtandalfer in charge of the ceremony nodded. "Then I pronounce you husband and wife. You may kiss."

If anything, that got an even bigger cheer from most of the room. Briony felt like joining in with them in that moment, because she would never get tired of kissing Kevin like this. Not having to hold back, her arms thrown around his neck and her mouth exploring his for what felt like forever.

It wasn't forever, of course. There were still so many other things they needed to do. There was the official crowning, which Sophie took charge of while Briony sat on the main throne. Her great aunt placed King Waltham's crown on her head. It was a little large, Briony noted. Probably, Vigor already had people working on producing a smaller one. He'd taken to seeing to so many of those small details as one of her new advisors and the head of her security.

Briony reached up, lifting the crown from her head as they'd practiced for this part of the ceremony. Kevin knelt before her, looking up at her with nothing but love.

Briony reached out to place the crown on his head before returning it to her own. Kevin had insisted on that piece of symbolism along with everyone else. While Briony wanted to crown him alongside her, he'd insisted that it should be clear that she was the queen, and he was simply her consort.

Queen. In theory, Briony had been the queen for a while now, but that had always felt like just a label. Something to call herself to get people to help against the vampires. A way of unlocking the power that they all needed to save themselves. They'd been so busy fighting that it hadn't felt like being the queen of Palisor was anything different.

Now, it was finally starting to sink in what being the ruler of a whole other world meant. Servants bowed or curtseyed to Briony in the halls when she went past. People wanted her to help make decisions about what to do with rebuilding spots the vampires had damaged. And there were the gates. One was open in the corner of the great hall now to let people back and forth between Palisor and Wicked. Briony had decided to keep one open permanently between the two spots. It would have to be guarded, but she wanted the people she cared about to be able to go back and forth between the worlds.

There was a party after the wedding. Actually, there had been a party going on for most of the week. Apparently, royal weddings were rare enough on Palisor that the people weren't going to settle for anything else. But this was the main party, a grand ball with hugtandalfer musicians playing stringed instruments and flutes, singing in ethereal voices and keeping up a steady rhythm on drums covered in dragon skin. Briony danced the first dance pressed tightly to Kevin, wishing that the moment would never end. Eventually though, she knew she had to talk to their guests.

She started with Maisy, Steve, and the others. Maisy hugged her.

"Congratulations! You look amazing!" Maisy stepped back and stared at her. "What does it feel like to finally be married to Kevin?"

"I was married to him before," Briony pointed out.

"I know, but doesn't this feel... I don't know, more official?"

It did, kind of, though the simple ceremony Vigor had presided over had felt so intimate and perfect. Honestly though, the thing that mattered was that they were married. The details of how it was done weren't important. Or rather, they were, but only from the point of view of her being Palisor's queen and having to put on a show.

Josh was next after Maisy. He slipped in before Briony could move on to her aunt or one of the waiting hugtandalfer representatives. That was good, because Briony had spent much of the last week hammering out a deal with him, and she wanted to make sure the werewolves' king remembered it.

"I'm still not sure you're doing the right thing, allowing so many vampires to live," Josh said.

"We've been through this," Briony pointed out. "And we have a deal, Josh. We *do* have a deal, don't we?"

Josh nodded. "Yes, we have a deal. I will allow the vampires of Wicked to live in peace. I will also help to hunt down any who kill humans. In return…"

"In return, your werewolves get to come into Palisor when they want," Briony said. "Some of them might even want to live here."

"Maybe." For a moment, Josh let the careful calculating façade slip a little. "Enjoy the rest of your wedding day, Briony."

"I will."

Josh slipped away into the crowd of well-wishers. By then though, Briony was looking elsewhere, for the one person she wanted to talk to more than anyone, but also the one person she was dreading talking to. She spotted him on the edge of the crowd and slipped after him, catching up with him at the entrance to an antechamber.

"Fallon-"

"Briony." He turned back to her. His face was unreadable. "I thought... I didn't want to get in the way on your wedding day."

"You know this is just for show. I'm already-"

"I know," Fallon said. He smiled. "And I thought I'd feel worse about that. But I can't hold a grudge. I'm not Pietre. I just want you to be happy."

That meant a lot, coming from him.

"I know you're not Pietre," Briony said.

"Is that why you did so much to stop me from dying? Me and the others? Don't get me wrong, I'm grateful. It's just... is keeping me, Jake and George alive worth all the destruction some vampires have wreaked? Is it worth what some of them will do in the future?"

Briony nodded. "Always. I won't kill the good to get rid of the evil. And that's not just for you. There are all the kids Pietre turned as well. They deserve a chance."

"Not all of them will take it."

"Some will. That's enough." Briony reached out to touch Fallon's arm. "You have a choice, too. Remember my promise?"

"Yes," Fallon said, "I remember. Can you do it? Can you actually transform a vampire to human?"

Briony nodded. "I think so. It will only work if they choose it, and I think I can only do a few at a time, but I can do it. Do you want it, Fallon? Do you want to be human again?"

Fallon hesitated. "I want it more than you could ever know, but..."

"But?" Briony echoed.

"But the young vampires Pietre turned need leadership. Some would want to be human again too, but not all of them, and if you couldn't turn them at once, what then? How many would give into their urges before you had a chance to turn them back. As much as I want to be human, they need me as a vampire."

"So you're going to stay as you are just to help them?" Briony asked. It was such a selfless thing for Fallon to do. She knew how much he wanted to be as he was.

Fallon shrugged. "If not me, then who? I'm the oldest of the vampires we know are good. If it's not me, then it would be George or Jake. Or none of us, and the new vampires become a threat to Wicked."

"Okay," Briony said. She knew he was right. It hurt that he was right, but he was. She smiled, and she thought she saw him start to reach out for her, but he stopped himself. They'd have to remember that now.

"There will be vampires who *will* want the transformation," Fallon said.

"I'll help them if I can," Briony promised.

"And maybe once everything has settled down, when they're all changed…"

They both knew that day would never come. There would always be more vampires, or those who wouldn't transform back.

"I'm going to keep the gates open," Briony said. "I want you to visit. Don't just stay in Wicked, Fallon."

Fallon nodded, but Kevin was there then, and Briony had to admit as he put an arm around her that she loved him being there. She turned to kiss him, just briefly. When she turned back, Fallon was gone.

"He didn't accept your offer did he?" Kevin guessed.

Briony shook her head. "He wants to be there for the new vampires,"

Kevin nodded. "That makes sense. And maybe... well, maybe he needs something like that. Something he can focus on."

Now that he couldn't focus on Briony. Neither of them said it, but it was there. Even so, it wasn't enough to make them any less happy in that moment. Briony could already feel the desire surging through Kevin, and the love. Always the love. She felt the same. She'd felt it from the start. She'd felt a lot for Fallon, but Kevin... she wouldn't have been able to let go of him if she tried.

And now she never had to. That was a good thought.

****

"Thinking good thoughts about the happy couple?"

Carol started slightly as her brother spoke. She should have sensed Josh sneaking up on her, but in the middle of the party, she'd lost track of who was where. Or maybe she'd just been too busy staring at Briony and Kevin to care.

"What do you care?"

"I'll always care, little sister," Josh said, putting an arm around her and gently steering her away from the antechamber. "You mustn't torture yourself about this."

Carol looked at him, trying to keep the pain out of her eyes and failing. "I loved him."

"But he wasn't for you, just as it turned out Briony wasn't for me." Josh shook his head. "There's someone out there for you, though. Someone who will make you happy, I'm sure of it."

Carol's eyes narrowed. "You don't need to treat me like some stupid little girl and tell me fairy stories, Josh. I'm an alpha wolf."

"I know," Josh said. "It doesn't make it any less true. One day, you *will* meet someone who's perfect for you, just as I'll meet my perfect queen. In the meantime... well, I think a lot is going to change for the pack."

"What do you mean?"

Josh smiled. "I'll tell you later. Now come on. I don't know about you, but I feel like heading back. Palisor is beautiful, but Wicked? Wicked is *home*."

This Concludes the Wicked Woods Series.

Stay tune for a new series featuring Fallon as the new master vampire of Wicked and the young woman who ends up challenging him in every way.

Wicked Ways

Coming in 2024

Kailin Gow

*From USA Today Bestselling Author
Kailin Gow*

BITTER FROST

All her life, Breena had always dreamed about fairies as though she lived amongst them... beautiful fairies living amongst mortals and living in Feyland. In her dreams, he was always there – the breathtakingly handsome but dangerous Winter Prince, Kian, who is her intended. Then she sees Kian, who seems intent on finding her and carrying her off to Feyland. If she is his intended, why does he seem to hate her and want her dead? And

Shifter: Wicked Woods #6

her best friend Logan has suddenly become protective.
Things are getting strange...

Kailin Gow

A FINAL WORD from the Author

Reasons Why?

I get asked this all the time, why do you interact with your readers so much?

1) The answer is simply because I see many of my readers as friends.

I'm a reader, too, and over the years, I've gotten to know some of you through Facebook, Twitter, or even at events I'm participating in. You have read my books, understood the story, and have come to love the characters in these stories as much as I do.

Over the years, I've gotten to know many of my readers. I share your pain when you lose a love one, congratulate you on victories, go through your birthdays and dramas at home and work. So you see, in other words, a lot of my readers have become friends of mine. You read my books, and even understand me like a friend understands a friend.

2) I know how reading can be time-consuming so I am pretty happy when a reader Facebook me and tells me she just read one of my books and she knows she'll be one of my biggest fans. I can't tell you how incredibly touched I am when someone tells me this. It literally brings tears to my eyes.

Not only does this feel incredible, and I am truly honored, but I want my readers to know from the bottom of my heart, this:

 3) You Make Me, an Author, feel Warm and Fuzzy, too!

When you love my books and even reach out to me to let me know how much you love my books or that it has touched you in some way, and even write a review about it, you can't imagine how happy that makes me. I'm only human you know. It makes me feel good about what I'm working hard for.

 4) My Readers are Not Only Interesting, but they are Fun, Smart, and Great to Hang Out with!

So, please don't be a stranger. Come on by and say "Hi" on Twitter, Facebook, or my blogs. And become a Facebook friend of mine and vice versa. I really do want to find out more about you, and consider it a great honor that you're a reader of mine.

From the bottom of my humble heart:

Kailin Gow

THANK YOU!

And if you enjoyed reading this book and want more books like this one get published, support this book and author by Letting others know.

Positive reviews and word-of-mouth is very much appreciated, too. And you never know, if my publisher like your glowing review so much, you may find it quoted in the next Loving Summer book.

That's one of the best support any author can ask for!

I love hearing from my readers! You can reach me at:

http://www.Kailingow.com

Other Books By Kailin Gow

Fantasy Romance Series
FROST SERIES
Age 15 and Up

Bitter Frost and The Wolf Fey
Forever Frost
Silver Frost
Frost Kisses
Midnight Frost
Frost Fire
Spring Frost
Enchanted Frost
Ring of Ice
Ring of Fire
The Fairy Letters

The Wolf Fey: Frost Series Spin-Off
Age 15 and Up

Kailin Gow

The Wolf Fey
The Red Wolf
Wolf Magic

The Fairy Rose Chronicles
(FROST Series that Takes Place 5 Years Earlier than the Bitter Frost Series)
AGE 9 and Up

The Fairy Rose
Fairy Fair (Fairy Rose Chronicles #2)
Pixies vs. Fairies (Fairy Rose Chronicles #3)

DESIRE
Age 17 and Up

Desire
Summer Wishes
Shattered
Passion

FADE
Age 15 and Up

FADE

Shifter: Wicked Woods #6

Falling
Forgotten
Fever

Wicked Woods Series
Age 15 and Up

Wicked Woods
Shimmer
Silver
Silence
Sight
Shifter

Alchemists Academy Series
Age 13 and Up

Stones to Ashes
Elemental Explosions
The Quantum Games
The Year of the Elite

Wordwick Games Series (An SAT-Prep Series)

Kailin Gow

<u>Age 15 and Up</u>

Rise of the Fire Tamer
The Ascension
The Return

Want More Edgy books for Teens and Up like this one?

Enter

Sparklesoup Teens

Sparklesoup.com/Teens

Where you will find edgy books for teens, young adults, and new adults that would make your heart pound, your skin crawl, and leave you wanting more…

Feed Your Reading Addiction